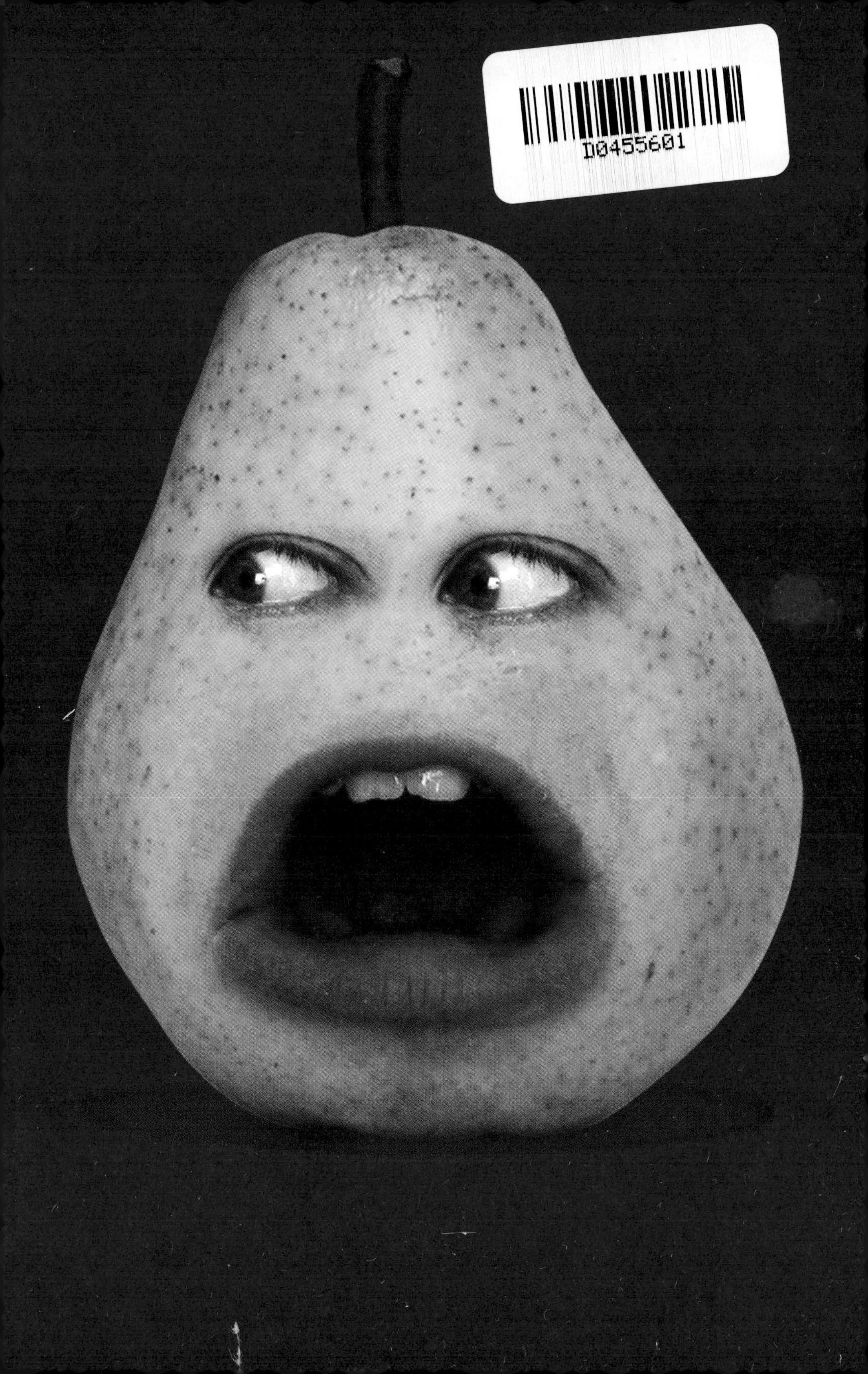

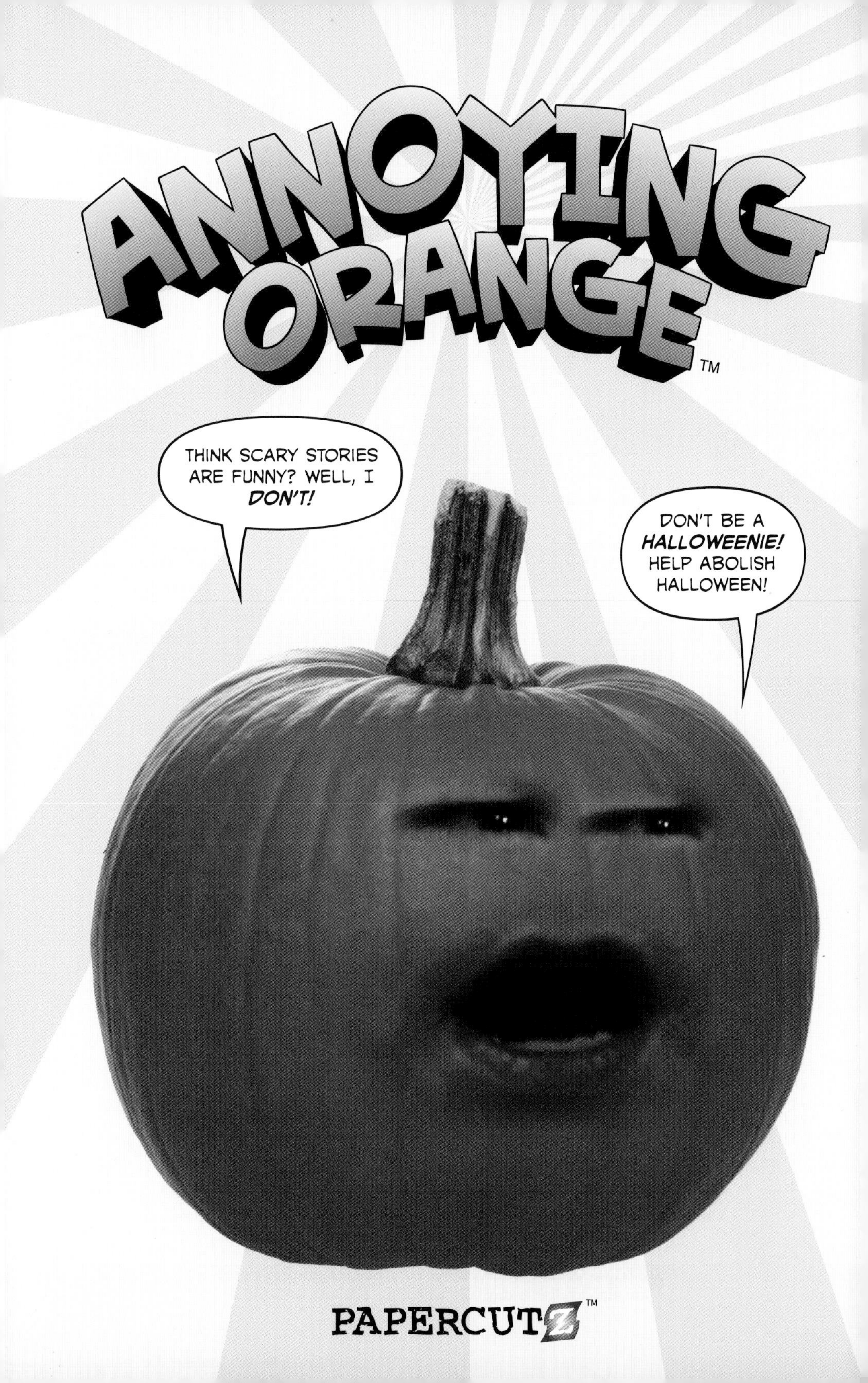
ANNOYING ORANGE™
THINK SCARY STORIES ARE FUNNY? WELL, I *DON'T!*
DON'T BE A ***HALLOWEENIE!*** HELP ABOLISH HALLOWEEN!
PAPERCUTZ™

ANNOYING ORANGE

AND OTHER GRAPHIC NOVELS AVAILABLE FROM PAPERCUTZ

COMING SOON!

ANNOYING ORANGE
SECRET AGENT ORANGE!

ANNOYING ORANGE
Graphic Novel #1
"Secret Agent Orange"

ANNOYING ORANGE

ANNOYING ORANGE
Graphic Novel #2
"Orange You Glad You're Not Me?"

ANNOYING ORANGE
PULPED FICTION

ANNOYING ORANGE
Graphic Novel #3
"Pulped Fiction"

ANNOYING ORANGE
TALES FROM THE CRISPER

ANNOYING ORANGE
Graphic Novel #4
"Tales from the Crisper"

ANNOYING ORANGE

ANNOYING ORANGE
Graphic Novel #5
"Transfarmers: Fruit Processors in Disguise!"

PAPERCUTZ SLICES
Harry Potty
AND THE DEATHLY BORING

PAPERCUTZ SLICES
Graphic Novel #1
"Harry Potty and the Deathly Boring"

PAPERCUTZ SLICES
AN ALL-NEW UNAUTHORIZED PARODY
breaking down

PAPERCUTZ SLICES
Graphic Novel #2
"breaking down"

PERCY JERKSON

PAPERCUTZ SLICES
Graphic Novel #3
"Percy Jerkson & The Ovolacto-vegetarians"

THE HUNGER PAINS
PETRUCHA
PARKER

PAPERCUTZ SLICES
Graphic Novel #4
"The Hunger Pains"

PAPERCUTZ SLICES
THE FARTING DEAD
PULL MY FINGER

PAPERCUTZ SLICES
Graphic Novel #5
"The Farting Dead"

ANNOYING ORANGE and PAPERCUTZ SLICES graphic novels, the print editions, are still available at booksellers everywhere.

Or order directly from Papercutz. ANNOYING ORANGE and PAPERCUTZ SLICES are available in paperback for $6.99 each; in hardcover for $10.99, except ANNOYING ORANGE #2, hardcover is $11.99, and ANNOYING ORANGE #3, #4, and #5 are $7.99 paperback, and $11.99 hardcover. Please add $4.00 for postage and handling for the first book, and add $1.00 for each additional book. Make check payable to NBM Publishing.

Send to: Papercutz, 160 Broadway, Suite 700, East Wing, New York, NY 10038

Or call 800-886-1223 between 9-5 EST, M-F. Visa, MC, and AmEx accepted.

www.papercutz.com

ANNOYING ORANGE and PAPERCUTZ SLICES graphic novels are also available digitally wherever e-books are sold.

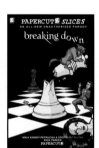

ANNOYING ORANGE™

TALES FROM THE CRISPER

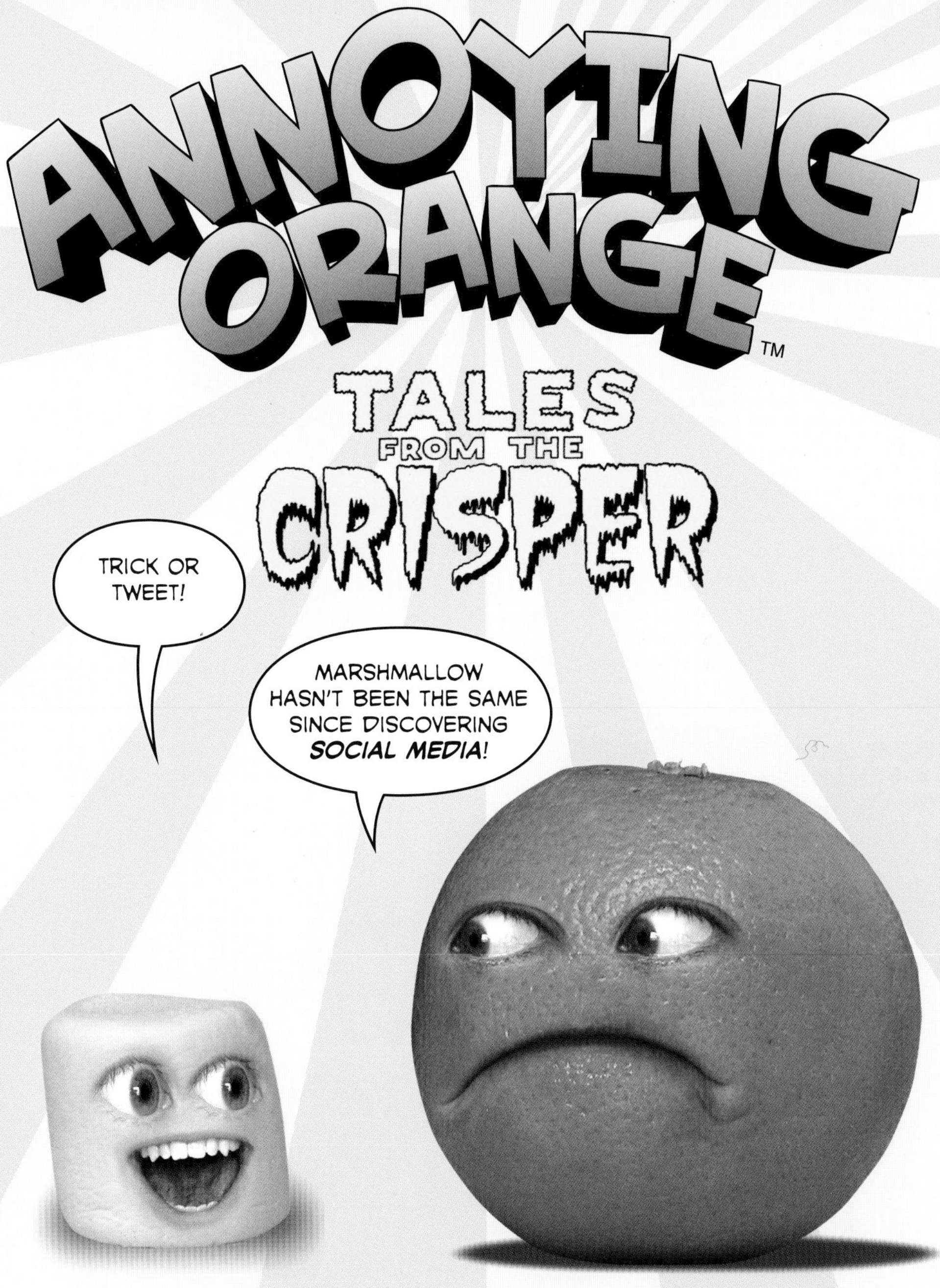
TRICK OR TWEET!
MARSHMALLOW HASN'T BEEN THE SAME SINCE DISCOVERING *SOCIAL MEDIA*!

Annoying Orange is created by DANE BOEDIGHEIMER

SCOTT SHAW! – Writer & Artist

MIKE KAZALEH – Writer & Artist

LAURIE E. SMITH – Colorist

PAPERCUTZ™
NEW YORK

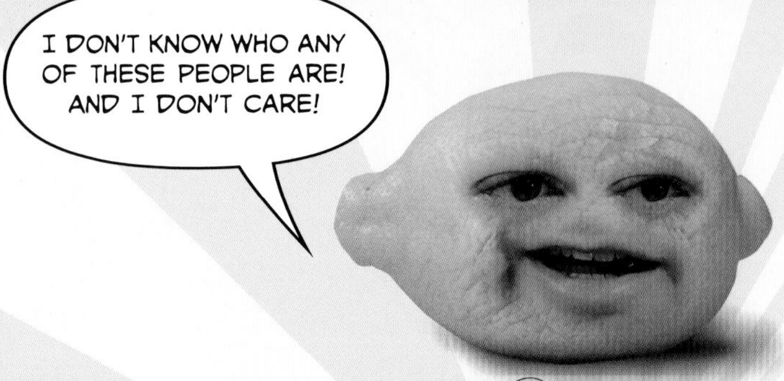
I DON'T KNOW WHO ANY OF THESE PEOPLE ARE! AND I DON'T CARE!

ANNOYING ORANGE™

#4 "Tales from the Crisper"

"Coffee Brake!" "Comic Con(flict)!" "That Ain't Hey!" "¡Frijoles, Frijoles, the Musical Fruit!"
"Annoying Role Call!" "Freshly-Picked (On) Grapefruit!" "Ava the Avacodo!"
"Dude, What's My Fruit Cart?" "A Tale of Two Citrus!" "Brothers of the Elastic Band!"
"Cosmic Comet Catastrophe!" "I Love Juicy!" "Praising Cane!"
"Just How Funny Are Talking Rocks and Minerals, Anyway?" "A Hairy Situation"
"You Can't Beat the Sweet!" "Super-Sour Seminar!" "Gus the Hippie Mushroom!"
"The Day the Fruit Stood Still!" "Crossword Fun with Fruit!" "Fun with Veggies Maze!"
"Fun with Nerville and Marshmallow Picture Puzzle!" and 3 "Phony Comicbook Ads!"
Scott Shaw! – Writer & Artist
Laurie E. Smith – Colorist
Janice Chiang – Letterer

"Chili Chiller"
Mike Kazaleh – Writer & Artist
Laurie E. Smith – Colorist
Tom Orzechowski – Letterer

Steve Mannion – Cover Artist
Laurie E. Smith – Cover Colorist
Tom Orzechowski – "Crisper" Title Letterering

Special thanks to:Gary Binkow, Tim Blankley, Dane Boedigheimer,
Spencer Grove, Teresa Harris, Reza Izad, Debra Joester, Polina Rey, Tom Sheppard
Production Coordinator: Beth Scorzato
Associate Editor: Michael Petranek
Jim Salicrup
Editor-in-Chief

ISBN: 978-1-59707-439-1 paperback edition
ISBN: 978-1-59707-440-7 hardcover edition

Printed in the USA
December 2013 by Lifetouch Printing
5126 Forest Hills Ct.
Loves Park, IL 61111

Papercutz books may be purchased for business or promotional use.
For information on bulk purchases please contact Macmillan Corporate
and Premium Sales Department at (800) 221-7945 x5442.

Distributed by Macmillan
First Printing

MEET THE FRUIT...

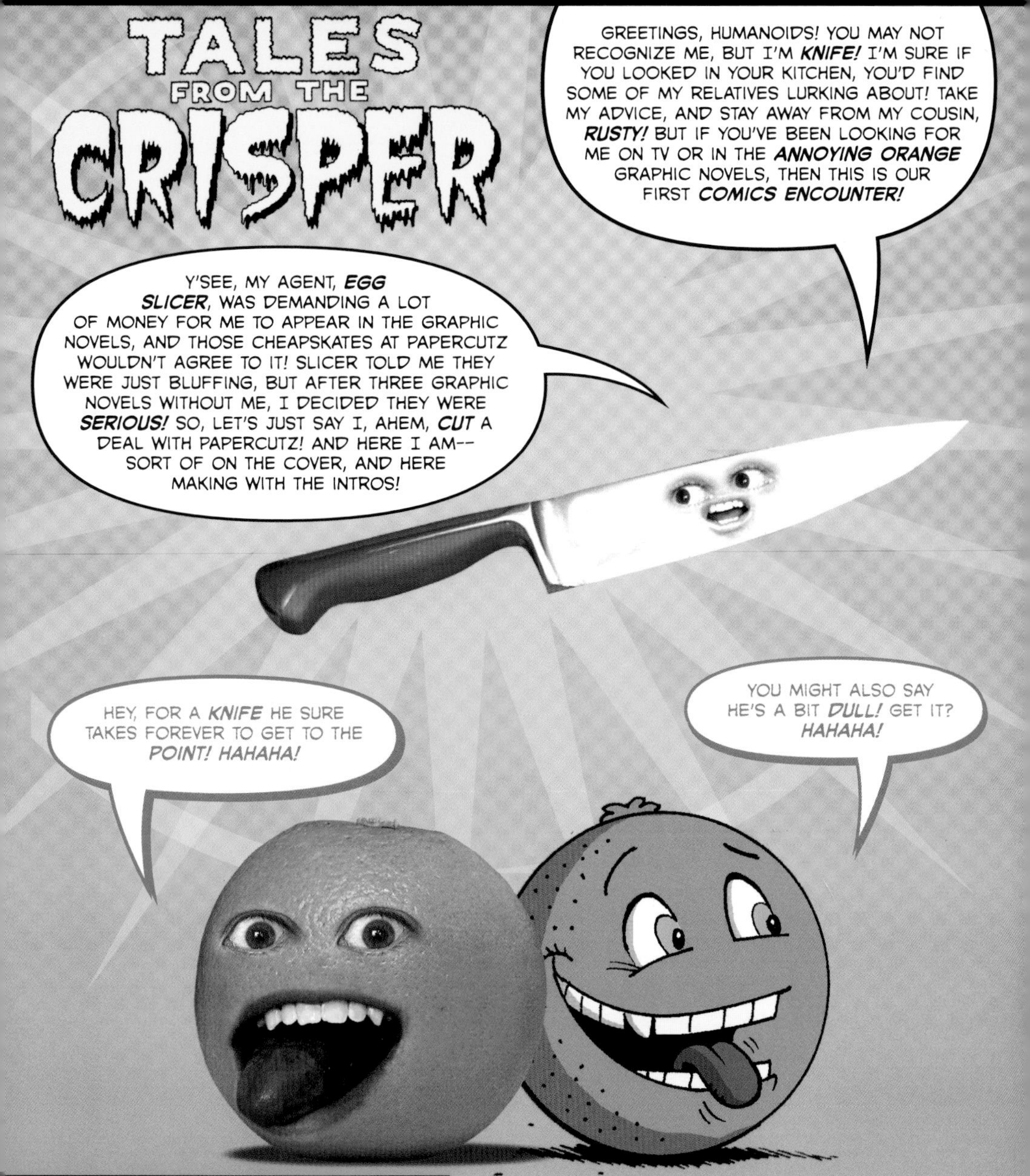
TALES FROM THE CRISPER
GREETINGS, HUMANOIDS! YOU MAY NOT RECOGNIZE ME, BUT I'M KNIFE! I'M SURE IF YOU LOOKED IN YOUR KITCHEN, YOU'D FIND SOME OF MY RELATIVES LURKING ABOUT! TAKE MY ADVICE, AND STAY AWAY FROM MY COUSIN, RUSTY! BUT IF YOU'VE BEEN LOOKING FOR ME ON TV OR IN THE ANNOYING ORANGE GRAPHIC NOVELS, THEN THIS IS OUR FIRST COMICS ENCOUNTER!
Y'SEE, MY AGENT, EGG SLICER, WAS DEMANDING A LOT OF MONEY FOR ME TO APPEAR IN THE GRAPHIC NOVELS, AND THOSE CHEAPSKATES AT PAPERCUTZ WOULDN'T AGREE TO IT! SLICER TOLD ME THEY WERE JUST BLUFFING, BUT AFTER THREE GRAPHIC NOVELS WITHOUT ME, I DECIDED THEY WERE SERIOUS! SO, LET'S JUST SAY I, AHEM, CUT A DEAL WITH PAPERCUTZ! AND HERE I AM-- SORT OF ON THE COVER, AND HERE MAKING WITH THE INTROS!
HEY, FOR A KNIFE HE SURE TAKES FOREVER TO GET TO THE POINT! HAHAHA!
YOU MIGHT ALSO SAY HE'S A BIT DULL! GET IT? HAHAHA!

ORANGE

As you can see, ORANGE is an orange who is ANNOYING! Whether on YouTube or The Cartoon Network, he's orange and annoying. The comics version is quite a cut-up, but still orange and annoying. There's really nothing more to know about him. Next!

HERE ARE SOME MORE CANDIDATES FOR A *FRUIT SALAD...!*

NOT EXACTLY *CUTTING-EDGE* HUMOR...

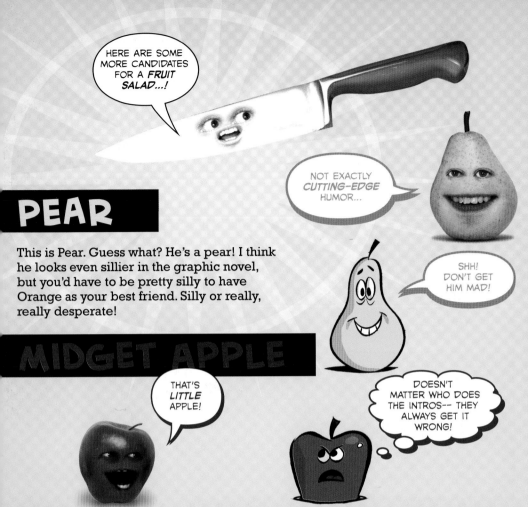

PEAR

This is Pear. Guess what? He's a pear! I think he looks even sillier in the graphic novel, but you'd have to be pretty silly to have Orange as your best friend. Silly or really, really desperate!

SHH! DON'T GET HIM MAD!

MIDGET APPLE

THAT'S *LITTLE* APPLE!

DOESN'T MATTER WHO DOES THE INTROS-- THEY ALWAYS GET IT WRONG!

As you can see the graphic novel MIDGET APPLE doesn't fall far from the Midget Apple tree! He's like a lot of guys I know, really hung up about his SIZE! He should get over it! Or maybe he'd like to be cut up into SLICES?! Hmm… maybe I should star in my own graphic novel series. They can call it PAPERCUTZ SLICES!*

GRANDPA LEMON

WHEN DID *KNIFE* BECOME SUCH A *SOUR PUSS?*

HEY! LOOK WHO'S TALKING!

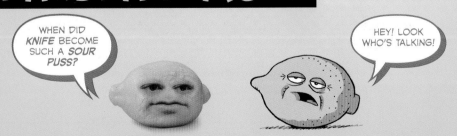

There's no fool, like an old FRUIT, and that's the best way to describe GRANDPA LEMON, whether onscreen or the printed page. So, do you like how my intros are short and sweet, or in this case, TART?

*Hey, we're not going to tell him we already have a series with that title (See page 2!) We may not be all that bright, but we're not STUPID! –*Jim Saladcrop, Editor*

JUST A FEW MORE INTROS LEFT BEFORE I *CUT* YOU LOOSE...!

PASSION FRUIT

I THINK *KNIFE* IS KINDA HOT!

THAT'S WHAT *BUTTER* SAID! HE DOES SEEM KINDA *SHARP!*

PASSION FRUIT seems a bit smarter than the rest of her fruity-friends, but when you realize she has an ORANGE CRUSH—and I don't mean the SOFT DRINK—well, there's just no accounting for taste! If you get my POINT!

MARSHMALLOW

I LIKE THAT *KNIFE* IS *SHINY!*

I LOVE *SHINY!* YAY!

My friend FONDUE FORK would probably like MARSHMALLOW… dipped in chocolate! Matter of fact, Marshmallow might even like it too. Marshmallow seems to like everything!

GRAPEFRUIT

I'M NOT AFRAID OF YOU, *KNIFE!*

YEAH, IT'S THE *HAND* THAT HOLDS YOU THAT I'M AFRAID OF!

The less said about GRAPEFRUIT the better. He loves to throw his WEIGHT around, but he's really a BIG BABY! Slicing him is no fun either— unless you like getting grapefruit juice squirted in your eyes! There-- done!

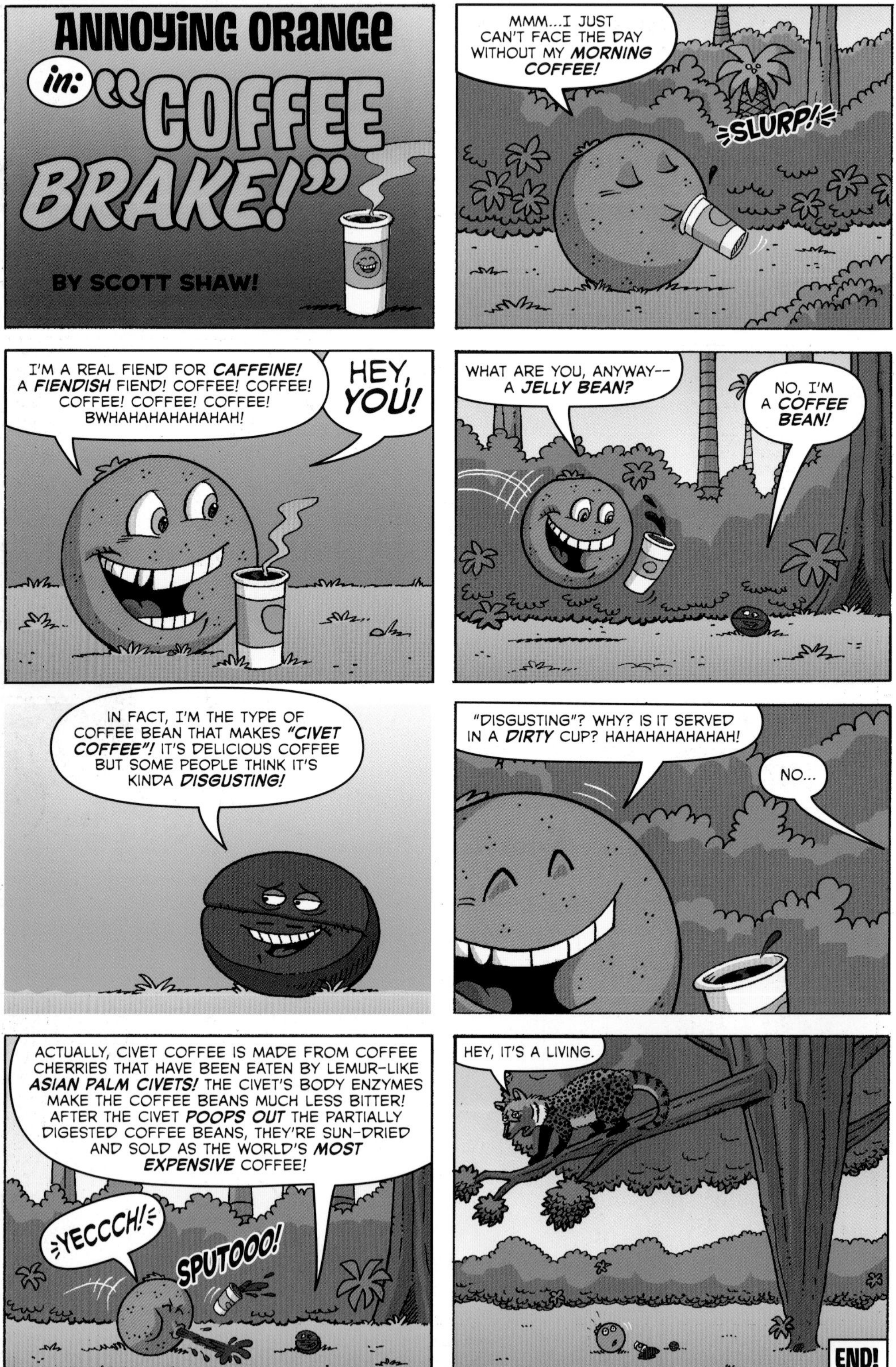
ANNOYING ORANGE
in: "COFFEE BRAKE!"
BY SCOTT SHAW!
MMM...I JUST CAN'T FACE THE DAY WITHOUT MY MORNING COFFEE!
SLURP!
I'M A REAL FIEND FOR CAFFEINE! A FIENDISH FIEND! COFFEE! COFFEE! COFFEE! COFFEE! COFFEE! BWHAHAHAHAHAHAH!
HEY, YOU!
WHAT ARE YOU, ANYWAY-- A JELLY BEAN?
NO, I'M A COFFEE BEAN!
IN FACT, I'M THE TYPE OF COFFEE BEAN THAT MAKES "CIVET COFFEE"! IT'S DELICIOUS COFFEE BUT SOME PEOPLE THINK IT'S KINDA DISGUSTING!
"DISGUSTING"? WHY? IS IT SERVED IN A DIRTY CUP? HAHAHAHAHAHAH!
NO...
ACTUALLY, CIVET COFFEE IS MADE FROM COFFEE CHERRIES THAT HAVE BEEN EATEN BY LEMUR-LIKE ASIAN PALM CIVETS! THE CIVET'S BODY ENZYMES MAKE THE COFFEE BEANS MUCH LESS BITTER! AFTER THE CIVET POOPS OUT THE PARTIALLY DIGESTED COFFEE BEANS, THEY'RE SUN-DRIED AND SOLD AS THE WORLD'S MOST EXPENSIVE COFFEE!
YECCCH!
SPUTOOO!
HEY, IT'S A LIVING.
END!

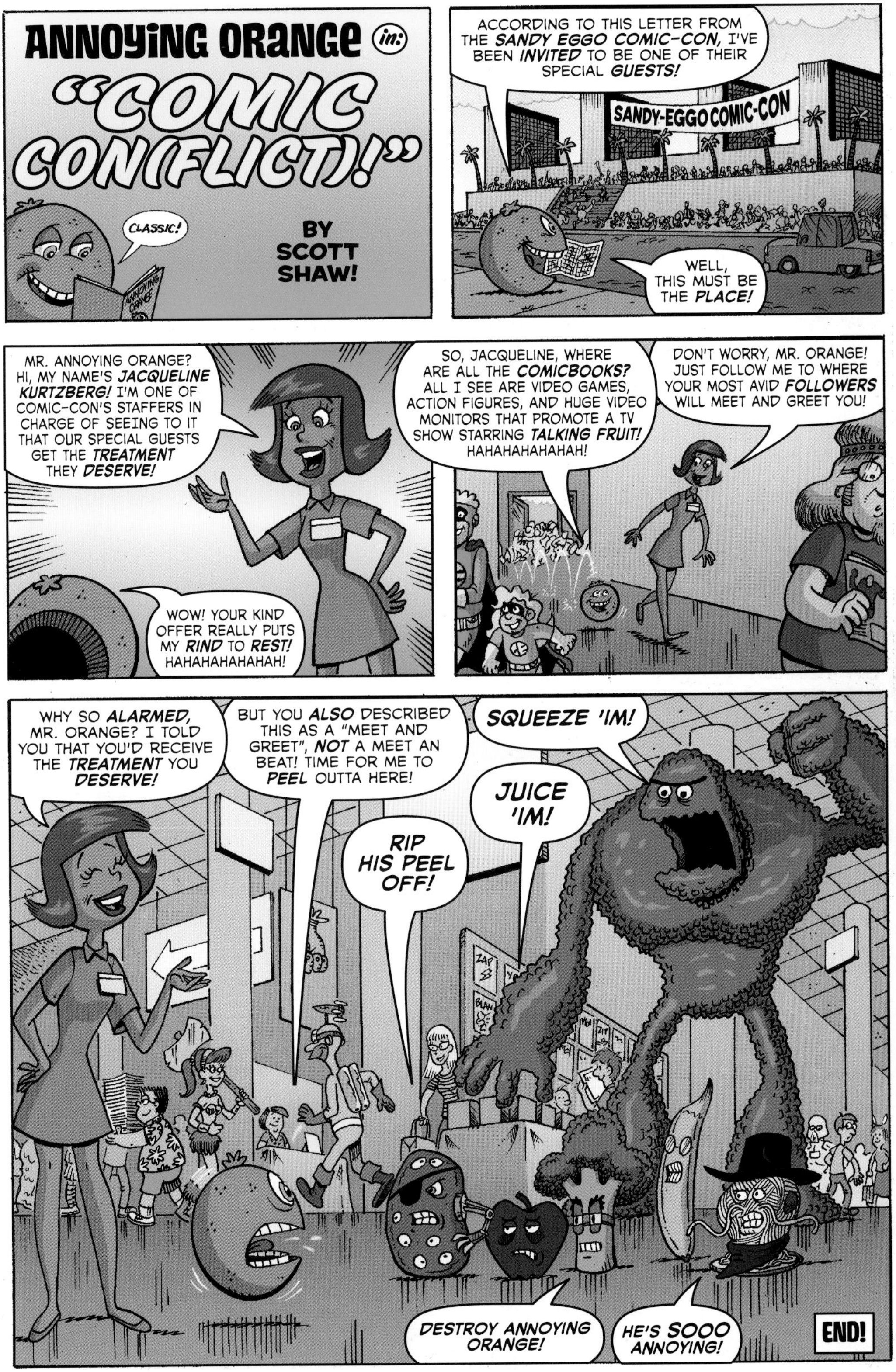
ANNOYING ORANGE in:
"COMIC CON(FLICT)!"
CLASSIC!
BY SCOTT SHAW!
ACCORDING TO THIS LETTER FROM THE SANDY EGGO COMIC-CON, I'VE BEEN INVITED TO BE ONE OF THEIR SPECIAL GUESTS!
SANDY-EGGO COMIC-CON
WELL, THIS MUST BE THE PLACE!
MR. ANNOYING ORANGE? HI, MY NAME'S JACQUELINE KURTZBERG! I'M ONE OF COMIC-CON'S STAFFERS IN CHARGE OF SEEING TO IT THAT OUR SPECIAL GUESTS GET THE TREATMENT THEY DESERVE!
WOW! YOUR KIND OFFER REALLY PUTS MY RIND TO REST! HAHAHAHAHAHAH!
SO, JACQUELINE, WHERE ARE ALL THE COMICBOOKS? ALL I SEE ARE VIDEO GAMES, ACTION FIGURES, AND HUGE VIDEO MONITORS THAT PROMOTE A TV SHOW STARRING TALKING FRUIT! HAHAHAHAHAHAH!
DON'T WORRY, MR. ORANGE! JUST FOLLOW ME TO WHERE YOUR MOST AVID FOLLOWERS WILL MEET AND GREET YOU!
WHY SO ALARMED, MR. ORANGE? I TOLD YOU THAT YOU'D RECEIVE THE TREATMENT YOU DESERVE!
BUT YOU ALSO DESCRIBED THIS AS A "MEET AND GREET", NOT A MEET AN BEAT! TIME FOR ME TO PEEL OUTTA HERE!
SQUEEZE 'IM!
JUICE 'IM!
RIP HIS PEEL OFF!
DESTROY ANNOYING ORANGE!
HE'S SOOO ANNOYING!
END!

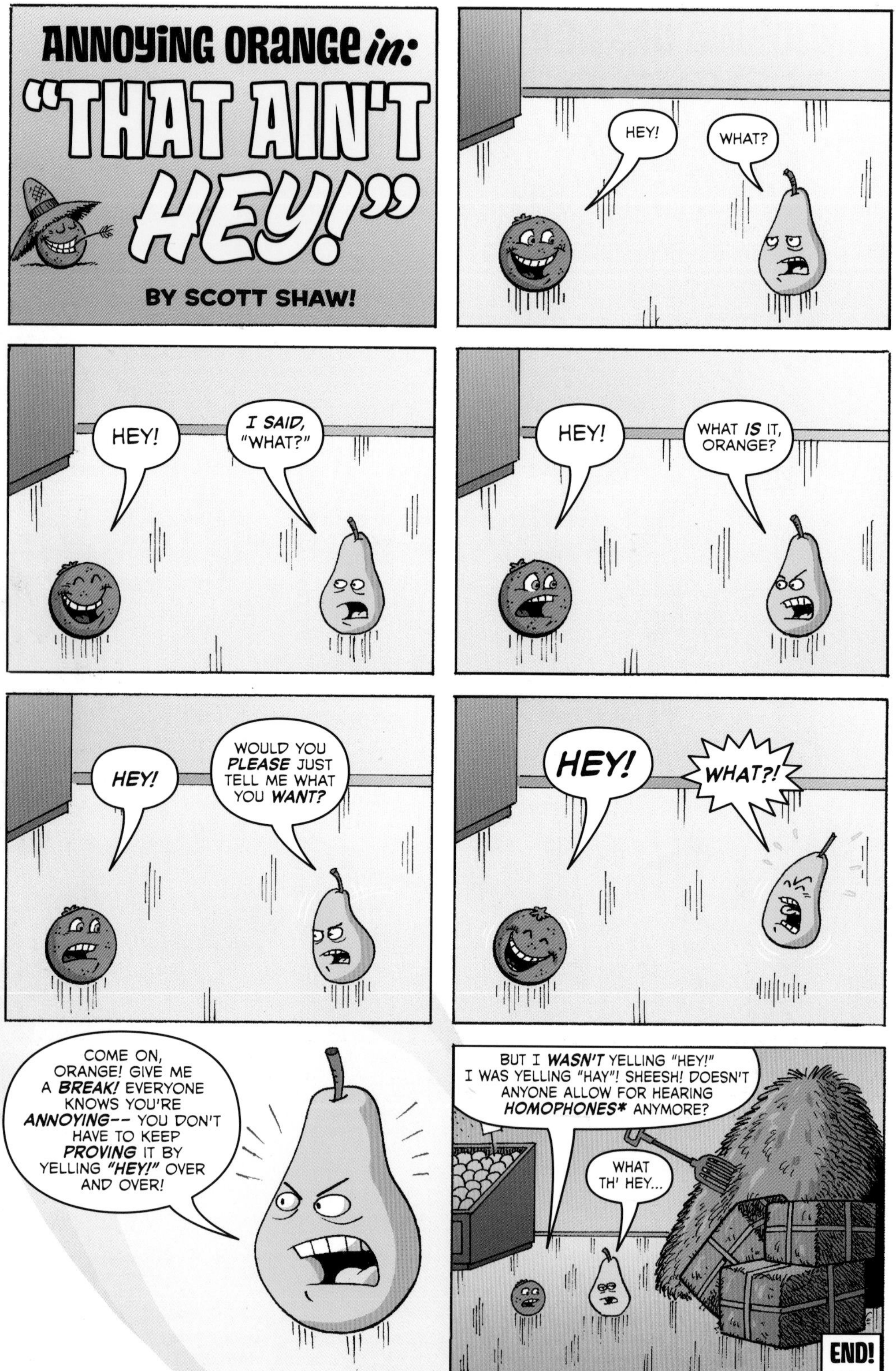

ANNOYING ORANGE in:
"THAT AIN'T HEY!"
BY SCOTT SHAW!
HEY!
WHAT?
HEY!
I SAID, "WHAT?"
HEY!
WHAT IS IT, ORANGE?
HEY!
WOULD YOU PLEASE JUST TELL ME WHAT YOU WANT?
HEY!
WHAT?!
COME ON, ORANGE! GIVE ME A BREAK! EVERYONE KNOWS YOU'RE ANNOYING-- YOU DON'T HAVE TO KEEP PROVING IT BY YELLING "HEY!" OVER AND OVER!
BUT I WASN'T YELLING "HEY!" I WAS YELLING "HAY"! SHEESH! DOESN'T ANYONE ALLOW FOR HEARING HOMOPHONES* ANYMORE?
WHAT TH' HEY...
END!

* LOOK IT UP, KIDS! -- JIM SALADCROP, EDITOR-IN-CHEESE

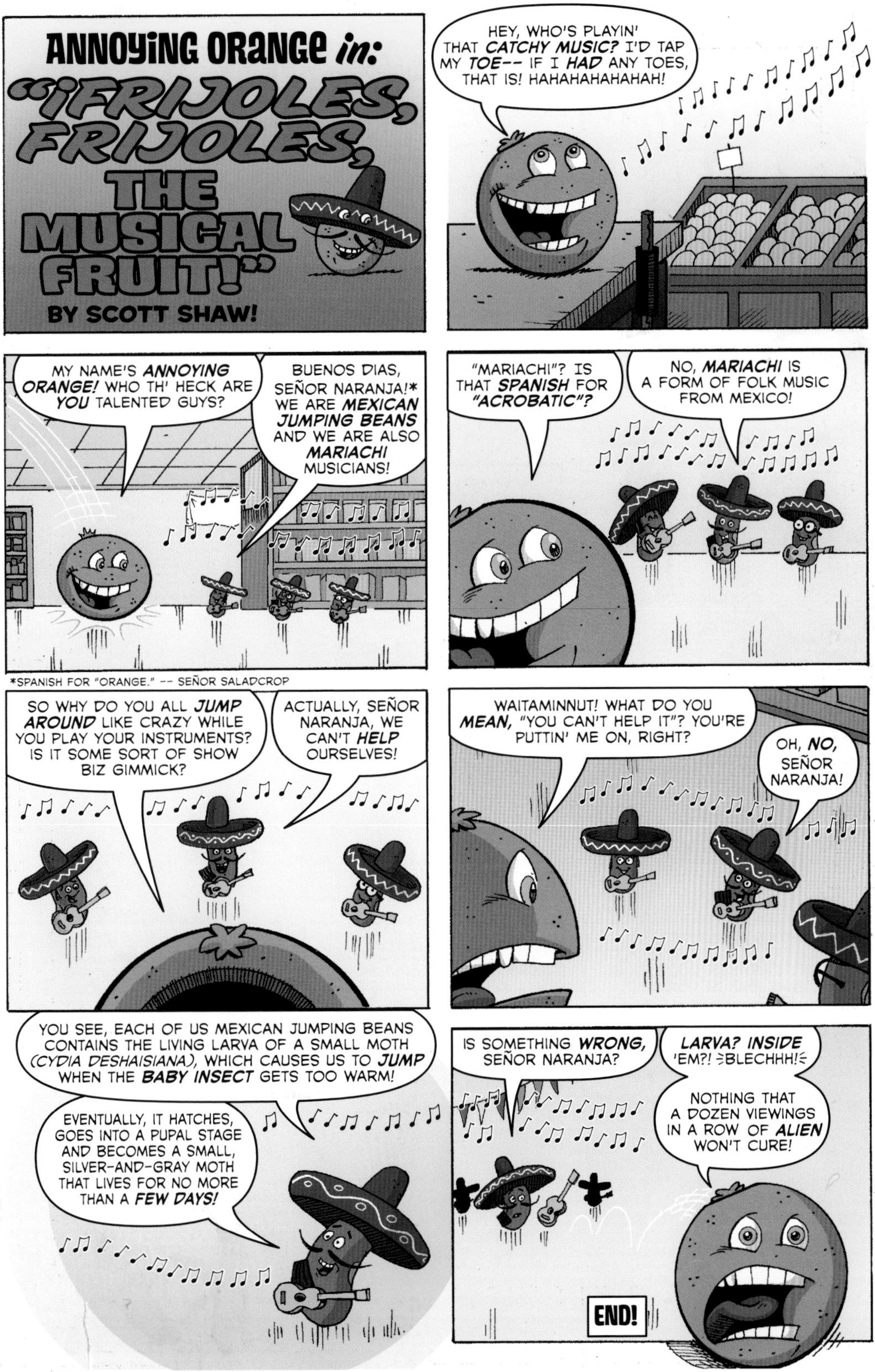

ANNOYING ORANGE in:
"¡FRIJOLES, FRIJOLES, THE MUSICAL FRUIT!"
BY SCOTT SHAW!
HEY, WHO'S PLAYIN' THAT CATCHY MUSIC? I'D TAP MY TOE-- IF I HAD ANY TOES, THAT IS! HAHAHAHAHAHAH!
MY NAME'S ANNOYING ORANGE! WHO TH' HECK ARE YOU TALENTED GUYS?
BUENOS DIAS, SEÑOR NARANJA!* WE ARE MEXICAN JUMPING BEANS AND WE ARE ALSO MARIACHI MUSICIANS!
*SPANISH FOR "ORANGE." -- SEÑOR SALADCROP
"MARIACHI"? IS THAT SPANISH FOR "ACROBATIC"?
NO, MARIACHI IS A FORM OF FOLK MUSIC FROM MEXICO!
SO WHY DO YOU ALL JUMP AROUND LIKE CRAZY WHILE YOU PLAY YOUR INSTRUMENTS? IS IT SOME SORT OF SHOW BIZ GIMMICK?
ACTUALLY, SEÑOR NARANJA, WE CAN'T HELP OURSELVES!
WAITAMINNUT! WHAT DO YOU MEAN, "YOU CAN'T HELP IT"? YOU'RE PUTTIN' ME ON, RIGHT?
OH, NO, SEÑOR NARANJA!
YOU SEE, EACH OF US MEXICAN JUMPING BEANS CONTAINS THE LIVING LARVA OF A SMALL MOTH (CYDIA DESHAISIANA), WHICH CAUSES US TO JUMP WHEN THE BABY INSECT GETS TOO WARM!
EVENTUALLY, IT HATCHES, GOES INTO A PUPAL STAGE AND BECOMES A SMALL, SILVER-AND-GRAY MOTH THAT LIVES FOR NO MORE THAN A FEW DAYS!
IS SOMETHING WRONG, SEÑOR NARANJA?
LARVA? INSIDE 'EM?! BLECHHH!
NOTHING THAT A DOZEN VIEWINGS IN A ROW OF ALIEN WON'T CURE!
END!

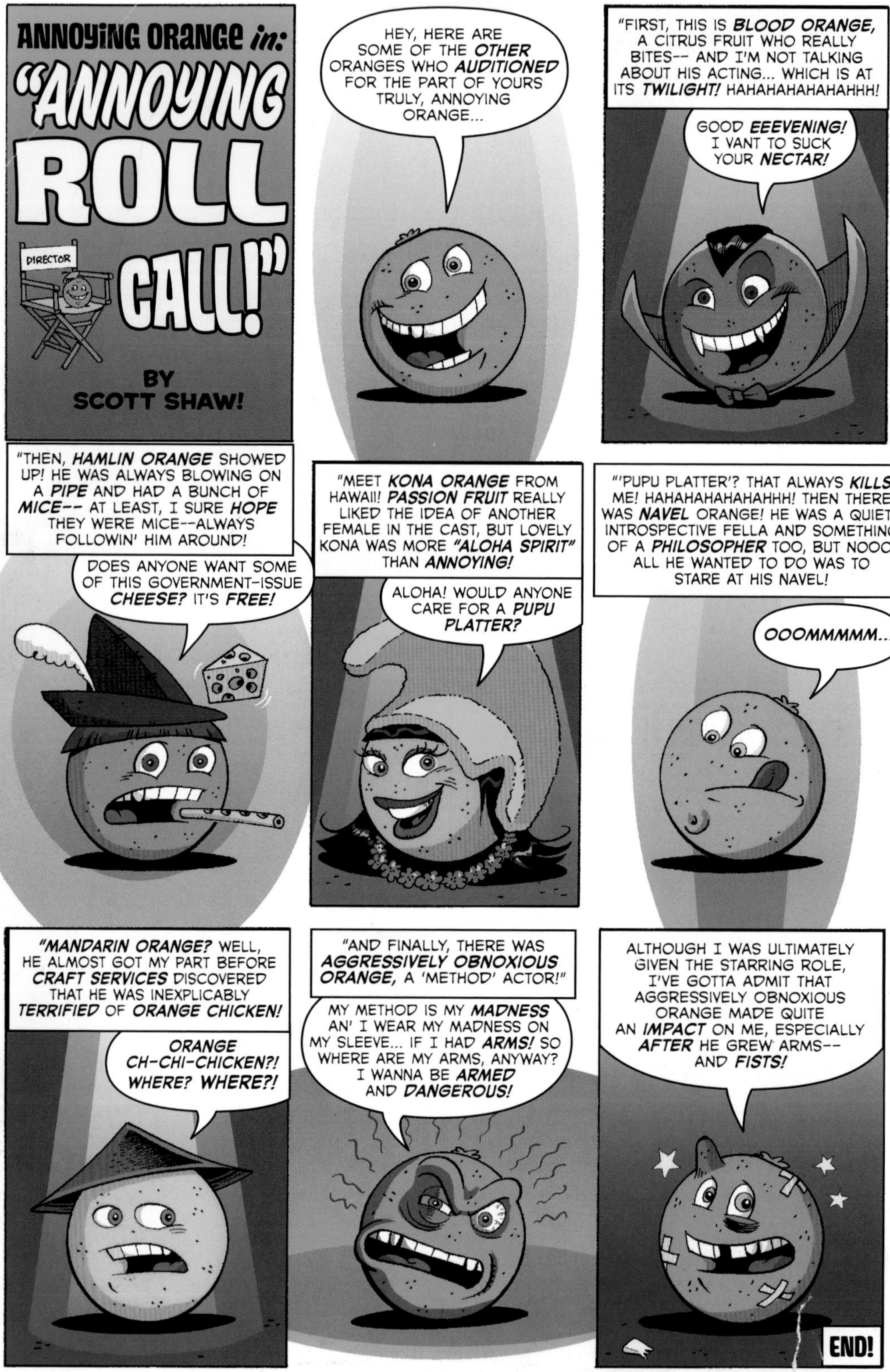
ANNOYING ORANGE in: "ANNOYING ROLL CALL!"
DIRECTOR
BY SCOTT SHAW!
HEY, HERE ARE SOME OF THE OTHER ORANGES WHO AUDITIONED FOR THE PART OF YOURS TRULY, ANNOYING ORANGE...
"FIRST, THIS IS BLOOD ORANGE, A CITRUS FRUIT WHO REALLY BITES-- AND I'M NOT TALKING ABOUT HIS ACTING... WHICH IS AT ITS TWILIGHT! HAHAHAHAHAHAHHH!
GOOD EEEVENING! I VANT TO SUCK YOUR NECTAR!
"THEN, HAMLIN ORANGE SHOWED UP! HE WAS ALWAYS BLOWING ON A PIPE AND HAD A BUNCH OF MICE-- AT LEAST, I SURE HOPE THEY WERE MICE--ALWAYS FOLLOWIN' HIM AROUND!
DOES ANYONE WANT SOME OF THIS GOVERNMENT-ISSUE CHEESE? IT'S FREE!
"MEET KONA ORANGE FROM HAWAII! PASSION FRUIT REALLY LIKED THE IDEA OF ANOTHER FEMALE IN THE CAST, BUT LOVELY KONA WAS MORE "ALOHA SPIRIT" THAN ANNOYING!
ALOHA! WOULD ANYONE CARE FOR A PUPU PLATTER?
"'PUPU PLATTER'? THAT ALWAYS KILLS ME! HAHAHAHAHAHAHHH! THEN THERE WAS NAVEL ORANGE! HE WAS A QUIET, INTROSPECTIVE FELLA AND SOMETHING OF A PHILOSOPHER TOO, BUT NOOO, ALL HE WANTED TO DO WAS TO STARE AT HIS NAVEL!
OOOMMMMM...
"MANDARIN ORANGE? WELL, HE ALMOST GOT MY PART BEFORE CRAFT SERVICES DISCOVERED THAT HE WAS INEXPLICABLY TERRIFIED OF ORANGE CHICKEN!
ORANGE CH-CHI-CHICKEN?! WHERE? WHERE?!
"AND FINALLY, THERE WAS AGGRESSIVELY OBNOXIOUS ORANGE, A 'METHOD' ACTOR!"
MY METHOD IS MY MADNESS AN' I WEAR MY MADNESS ON MY SLEEVE... IF I HAD ARMS! SO WHERE ARE MY ARMS, ANYWAY? I WANNA BE ARMED AND DANGEROUS!
ALTHOUGH I WAS ULTIMATELY GIVEN THE STARRING ROLE, I'VE GOTTA ADMIT THAT AGGRESSIVELY OBNOXIOUS ORANGE MADE QUITE AN IMPACT ON ME, ESPECIALLY AFTER HE GREW ARMS-- AND FISTS!
END!

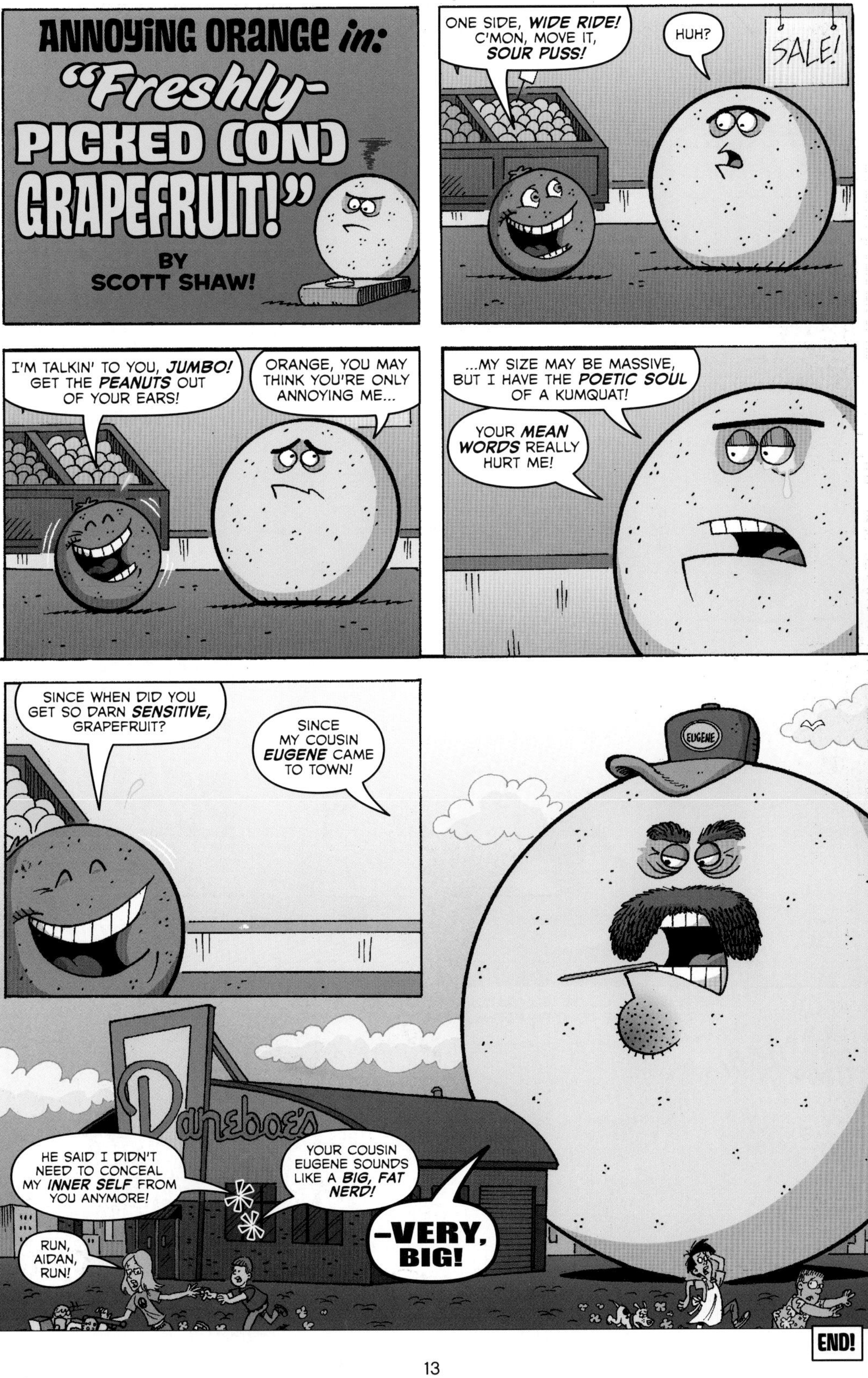
ANNOYING ORANGE in:
"Freshly-PICKED (CON) GRAPEFRUIT!"
BY SCOTT SHAW!
ONE SIDE, WIDE RIDE! C'MON, MOVE IT, SOUR PUSS!
HUH?
SALE!
I'M TALKIN' TO YOU, JUMBO! GET THE PEANUTS OUT OF YOUR EARS!
ORANGE, YOU MAY THINK YOU'RE ONLY ANNOYING ME...
...MY SIZE MAY BE MASSIVE, BUT I HAVE THE POETIC SOUL OF A KUMQUAT!
YOUR MEAN WORDS REALLY HURT ME!
SINCE WHEN DID YOU GET SO DARN SENSITIVE, GRAPEFRUIT?
SINCE MY COUSIN EUGENE CAME TO TOWN!
EUGENE
HE SAID I DIDN'T NEED TO CONCEAL MY INNER SELF FROM YOU ANYMORE!
YOUR COUSIN EUGENE SOUNDS LIKE A BIG, FAT NERD!
–VERY, BIG!
RUN, AIDAN, RUN!
END!

PEAR in: "AVA THE AVOCADO!"
BY SCOTT SHAW!
HI THERE, I'M PEAR! WHAT'S YOUR NAME, CUTE-FRUIT?
I'M AVA THE AVOCADO-- WE'RE THE FRUIT THAT'S KNOWN AS ONE OF THE WORLD'S HEALTHIEST FOODS!
AN AVOCADO? I THOUGHT YOU WERE ANOTHER PEAR!
WELL, IT IS TRUE THAT SOME PEOPLE CALL US "ALLIGATOR PEARS"!
I'LL BET THAT'S BECAUSE YOUR SKIN HAS A SIMILAR PATTERN TO AN ALLIGATOR'S LEATHERY HIDE, RIGHT?
THAT'S A GOOD GUESS, MR. PEAR, BUT YOU'RE NOT EVEN CLOSE! GIGGLE!
OKAY, PLEASE TELL ME--
ROARRR!
HOLY GUACAMOLE!
SOME PEOPLE CALL US "ALLIGATOR PEARS" BECAUSE MOST OF US AVOCADOS LIKE TO KEEP PET ALLIGATORS LIKE ALBERT HERE.
ROARRR!
ADIOS, ADORABLE AVA!
YOU MAY BE ONE OF THE WORLD'S HEALTHIEST FRUITS BUT ALBERT HERE HAS GOTTA BE ONE OF THE WORLD'S LEAST HEALTHY PETS-- AT LEAST FOR ME! SEE YOU LATER, ALLIGATOR!
END!

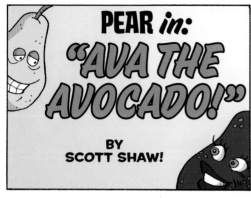

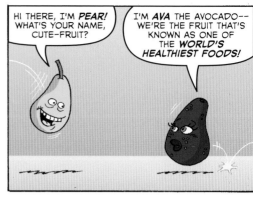

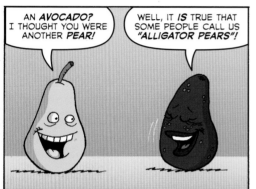

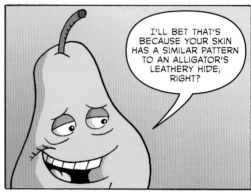

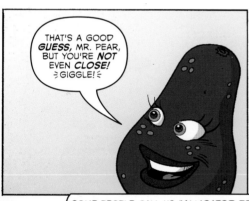

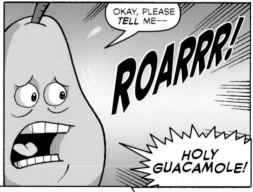

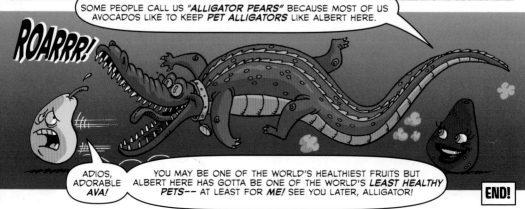

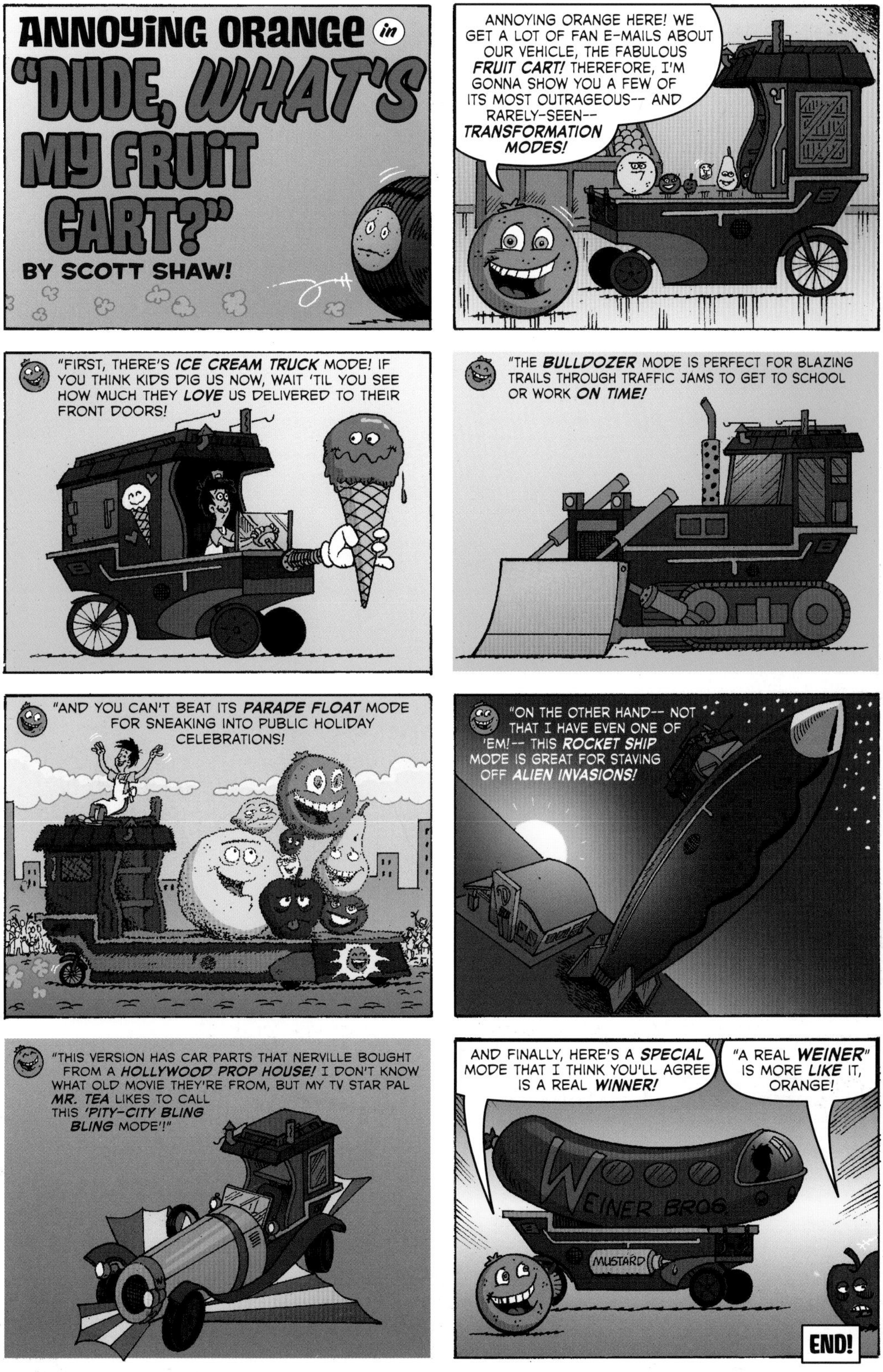

ANNOYING ORANGE in
"DUDE, WHAT'S MY FRUIT CART?"
BY SCOTT SHAW!
ANNOYING ORANGE HERE! WE GET A LOT OF FAN E-MAILS ABOUT OUR VEHICLE, THE FABULOUS FRUIT CART! THEREFORE, I'M GONNA SHOW YOU A FEW OF ITS MOST OUTRAGEOUS-- AND RARELY-SEEN-- TRANSFORMATION MODES!
"FIRST, THERE'S ICE CREAM TRUCK MODE! IF YOU THINK KIDS DIG US NOW, WAIT 'TIL YOU SEE HOW MUCH THEY LOVE US DELIVERED TO THEIR FRONT DOORS!
"THE BULLDOZER MODE IS PERFECT FOR BLAZING TRAILS THROUGH TRAFFIC JAMS TO GET TO SCHOOL OR WORK ON TIME!
"AND YOU CAN'T BEAT ITS PARADE FLOAT MODE FOR SNEAKING INTO PUBLIC HOLIDAY CELEBRATIONS!
"ON THE OTHER HAND-- NOT THAT I HAVE EVEN ONE OF 'EM!-- THIS ROCKET SHIP MODE IS GREAT FOR STAVING OFF ALIEN INVASIONS!
"THIS VERSION HAS CAR PARTS THAT NERVILLE BOUGHT FROM A HOLLYWOOD PROP HOUSE! I DON'T KNOW WHAT OLD MOVIE THEY'RE FROM, BUT MY TV STAR PAL MR. TEA LIKES TO CALL THIS 'PITY-CITY BLING BLING MODE'!"
AND FINALLY, HERE'S A SPECIAL MODE THAT I THINK YOU'LL AGREE IS A REAL WINNER!
"A REAL WEINER" IS MORE LIKE IT, ORANGE!
WEINER BROS
MUSTARD
END!

ANNOYING ORANGE and the FRUIT CART GANG in:
"A TALE OF TWO CITRUS!"
BY SCOTT SHAW!

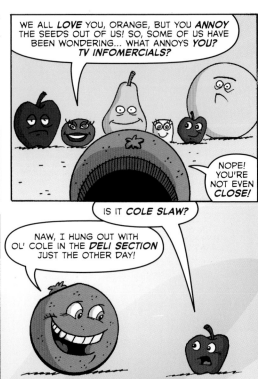

WE ALL *LOVE* YOU, ORANGE, BUT YOU *ANNOY* THE SEEDS OUT OF US! SO, SOME OF US HAVE BEEN WONDERING... WHAT ANNOYS *YOU*? TV INFOMERCIALS?

NOPE! YOU'RE NOT EVEN *CLOSE*!

IS IT *COLE SLAW?*

NAW, I HUNG OUT WITH OL' COLE IN THE *DELI SECTION* JUST THE OTHER DAY!

HOW ABOUT *COUNTRY-WESTERN MUSIC?*

SORRY, PAL! YOU OUGHTTA SEE ME CUT A RUG IN MY *COWBOY BOOTS!*

WHAT ABOUT *NASCAR RACES?*

ARE YOU *KIDDIN'?* NO ONE LOVES *EXPLOSIONS* AND DODGIN' *LOOSE RACE CAR PARTS* MORE THAN *I!*

SOMETHING TELLS ME THAT A BAD CASE OF *LOCKJAW* WOULD REALLY ANNOY YOU, ORANGE!

NOT REALLY! AFTER ALL, I COULD DRIVE YOU ALL NUTSO WITH SUSPENSE WONDERING *WHEN* I COULD SPEAK AGAIN!

HOW ABOUT *YOU*, MARSHMALLOW? WANNA VENTURE A *GUESS?*

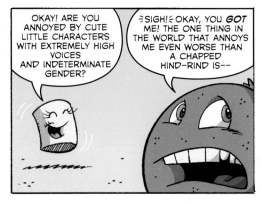

OKAY! ARE YOU ANNOYED BY CUTE LITTLE CHARACTERS WITH EXTREMELY HIGH VOICES AND INDETERMINATE GENDER?

≷SIGH!≷ OKAY, YOU *GOT* ME! THE ONE THING IN THE WORLD THAT ANNOYS ME EVEN WORSE THAN A CHAPPED HIND-RIND IS--

--CUTESY TANGERINE!

HI, EVERYBODY! IT'S *ME*, THE TEENSY, TINY, EASY-PEELIN' FRUIT THAT'S *TOO SWEET* TO EAT!

≷WHEW!≷ AT LEAST ORANGE *WASN'T* TALKING ABOUT *ME!*

YAY!

END!

16

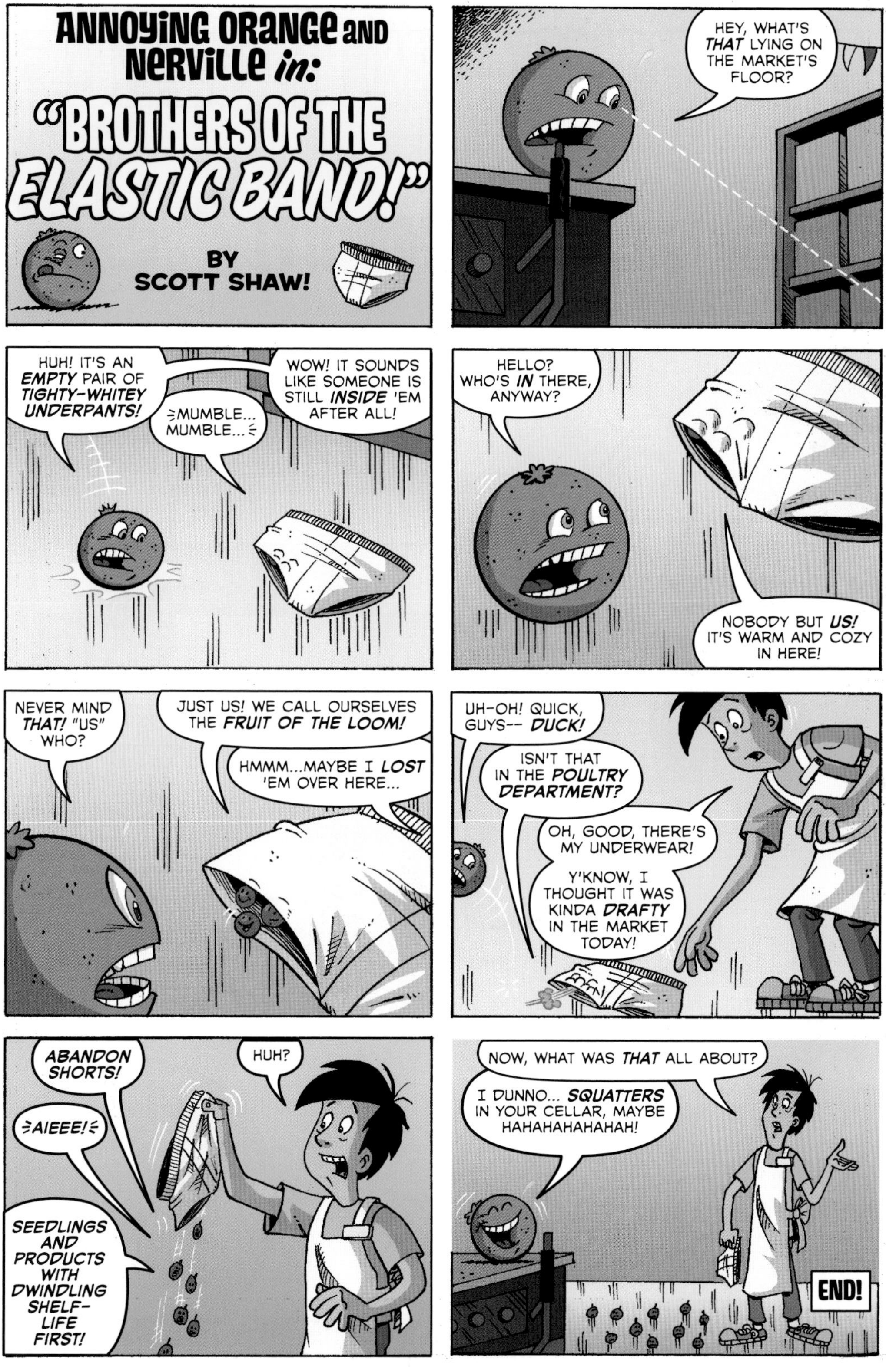
ANNOYING ORANGE AND NERVILLE in:
"BROTHERS OF THE ELASTIC BAND!"
BY SCOTT SHAW!
HEY, WHAT'S THAT LYING ON THE MARKET'S FLOOR?
HUH! IT'S AN EMPTY PAIR OF TIGHTY-WHITEY UNDERPANTS!
MUMBLE... MUMBLE...
WOW! IT SOUNDS LIKE SOMEONE IS STILL INSIDE 'EM AFTER ALL!
HELLO? WHO'S IN THERE, ANYWAY?
NOBODY BUT US! IT'S WARM AND COZY IN HERE!
NEVER MIND THAT! "US" WHO?
JUST US! WE CALL OURSELVES THE FRUIT OF THE LOOM!
HMMM...MAYBE I LOST 'EM OVER HERE...
UH-OH! QUICK, GUYS-- DUCK!
ISN'T THAT IN THE POULTRY DEPARTMENT?
OH, GOOD, THERE'S MY UNDERWEAR!
Y'KNOW, I THOUGHT IT WAS KINDA DRAFTY IN THE MARKET TODAY!
ABANDON SHORTS!
HUH?
AIEEE!
SEEDLINGS AND PRODUCTS WITH DWINDLING SHELF-LIFE FIRST!
NOW, WHAT WAS THAT ALL ABOUT?
I DUNNO... SQUATTERS IN YOUR CELLAR, MAYBE HAHAHAHAHAHAH!
END!

CROSSWORD PUZZLE FUN --

with GRAPEFRUIT!

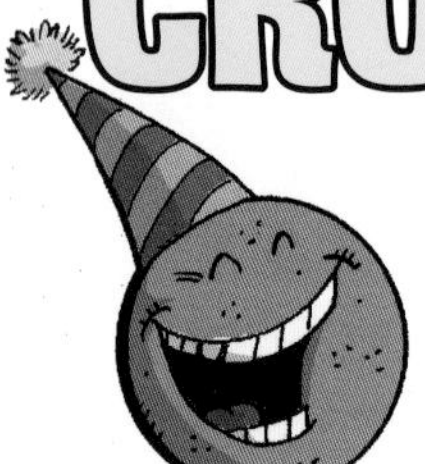

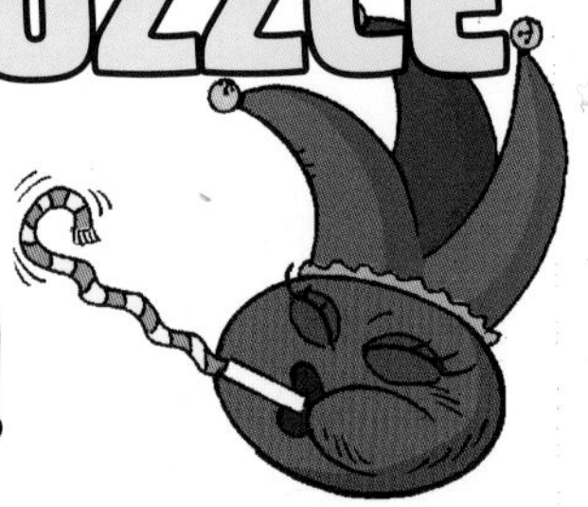

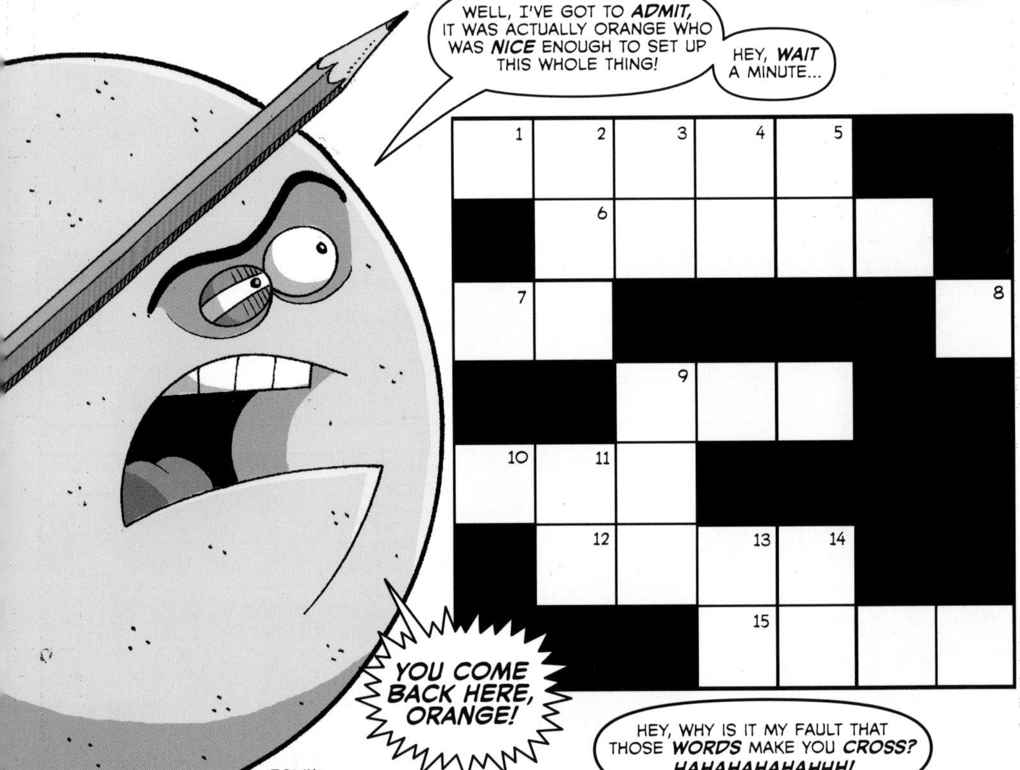

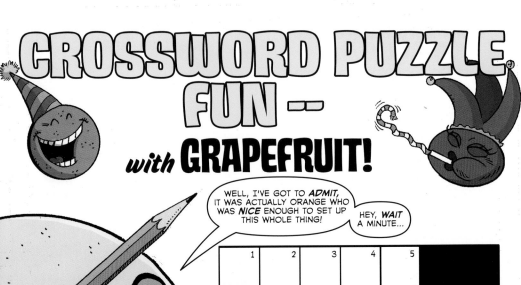

WELL, I'VE GOT TO *ADMIT,* IT WAS ACTUALLY ORANGE WHO WAS *NICE* ENOUGH TO SET UP THIS WHOLE THING!
HEY, *WAIT* A MINUTE...
1
2
3
4
5
6
7
8
9
10
11
12
13
14
15
YOU COME BACK HERE, ORANGE!

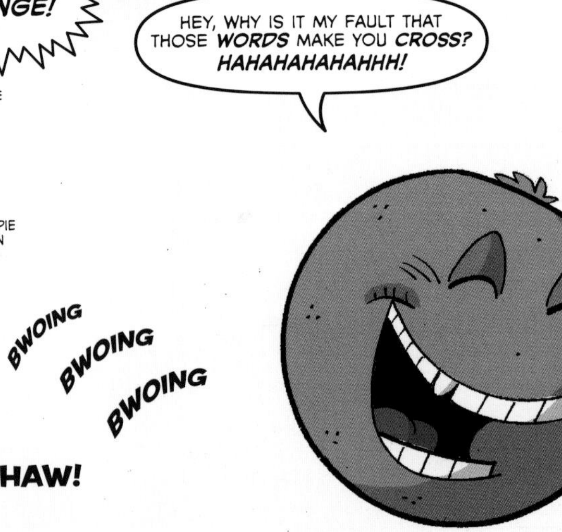

HEY, WHY IS IT MY FAULT THAT THOSE *WORDS* MAKE YOU *CROSS?* *HAHAHAHAHAHHH!*
BWOING
BWOING
BWOING

ACROSS:

1. ONE OF BUNCHES OF THEM THAT GROW ON VINES
6. A BOUNTY OF HARVESTING BUT NOT A VEGETABLE
7. PRESENT-TENSE OF "WAS"
8. SINGULAR VOWEL
9. LARGE
10. HEAVY-SET
12. TART; THE OPPOSITE OF SWEET
15. AFFECTIONATE NAME FOR A KITTY-CAT

DOWN:

2. ABBREVIATION FOR RENEWABLE FUEL STANDARD
3. WHAT PIRATES SAY
4. WHAT YOU SAY IF YOU SMELL DURIAN
5. ABBREVIATION OF WHAT OUT-OF-WORK CANADIANS COLLECT
9. ABBREVIATION OF GUS THE HIPPIE MUSHROOM'S FAVORITE CANADIAN ROCK BAND
11. ADVERB MEANING TO THE SAME DEGREE, AMOUNT, OR EXTENT
13. OPPOSITE OF DOWN
14. HOW TEXTERS SPELL "ARE YOU"

ANSWERS ON PAGE 55

WRITTEN AND DRAWN BY SCOTT SHAW!

(PHONY ADVERTISEMENT)

HEY, KIDS!

GROW YOUR OWN MUTANT BRUSSELS SPROUTS IN YOUR SPARE TIME! SELL BRUSSELS SPROUTS SEEDS TO YOUR FRIENDS AND FAMILY! WIN VALUABLE PRIZES!

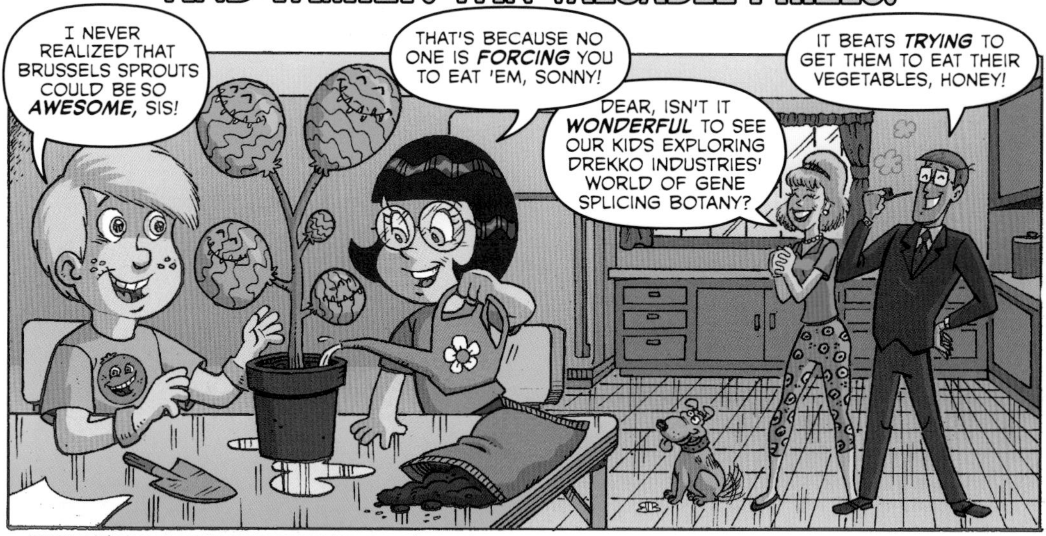
I NEVER REALIZED THAT BRUSSELS SPROUTS COULD BE SO ***AWESOME,*** SIS!
THAT'S BECAUSE NO ONE IS ***FORCING*** YOU TO EAT 'EM, SONNY!
IT BEATS ***TRYING*** TO GET THEM TO EAT THEIR VEGETABLES, HONEY!
DEAR, ISN'T IT ***WONDERFUL*** TO SEE OUR KIDS EXPLORING DREKKO INDUSTRIES' WORLD OF GENE SPLICING BOTANY?

Note: Mutant Brussels sprouts seeds may not grow as large as these – your results may vary!

Yes, you, too, can be the scientific mastermind who mutates living plants to obey your every whim, with DREKKO INDUSTRIES' new HOME BOTANY LABORATORY! Turn your salad into the vegetable slave of tomorrow, thanks to Drekko's application of the latest technologies in renegade crop growth! Just fill out the coupon below, mail it and in six weeks, you'll be a veritable Dr. Moreau!

YOU CAN EARN THESE GREAT PRIZES, TOO!

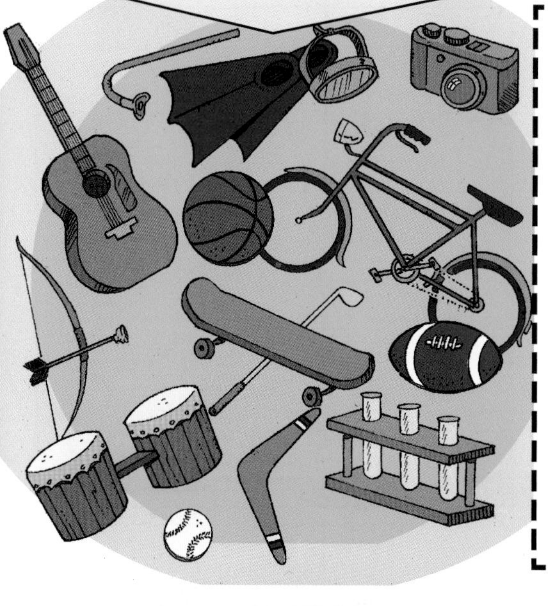

☐ **Yes,** I can't wait to grow my own mutant Brussels sprouts in my own spare time and sell Brussels sprouts seeds to my friends and family and win valuable prizes!

NAME: ______________________

ADDRESS: ______________________

______________________ ZIP CODE: ________

Send this completed form along with $29.95 cash, plus $5.00 to cover postage and handling, to:

VEG-O-MANIC, INC.
19130 Duzzantexist Avenue
Fakeville, NY 11237

***Written and drawn by* SCOTT SHAW!**

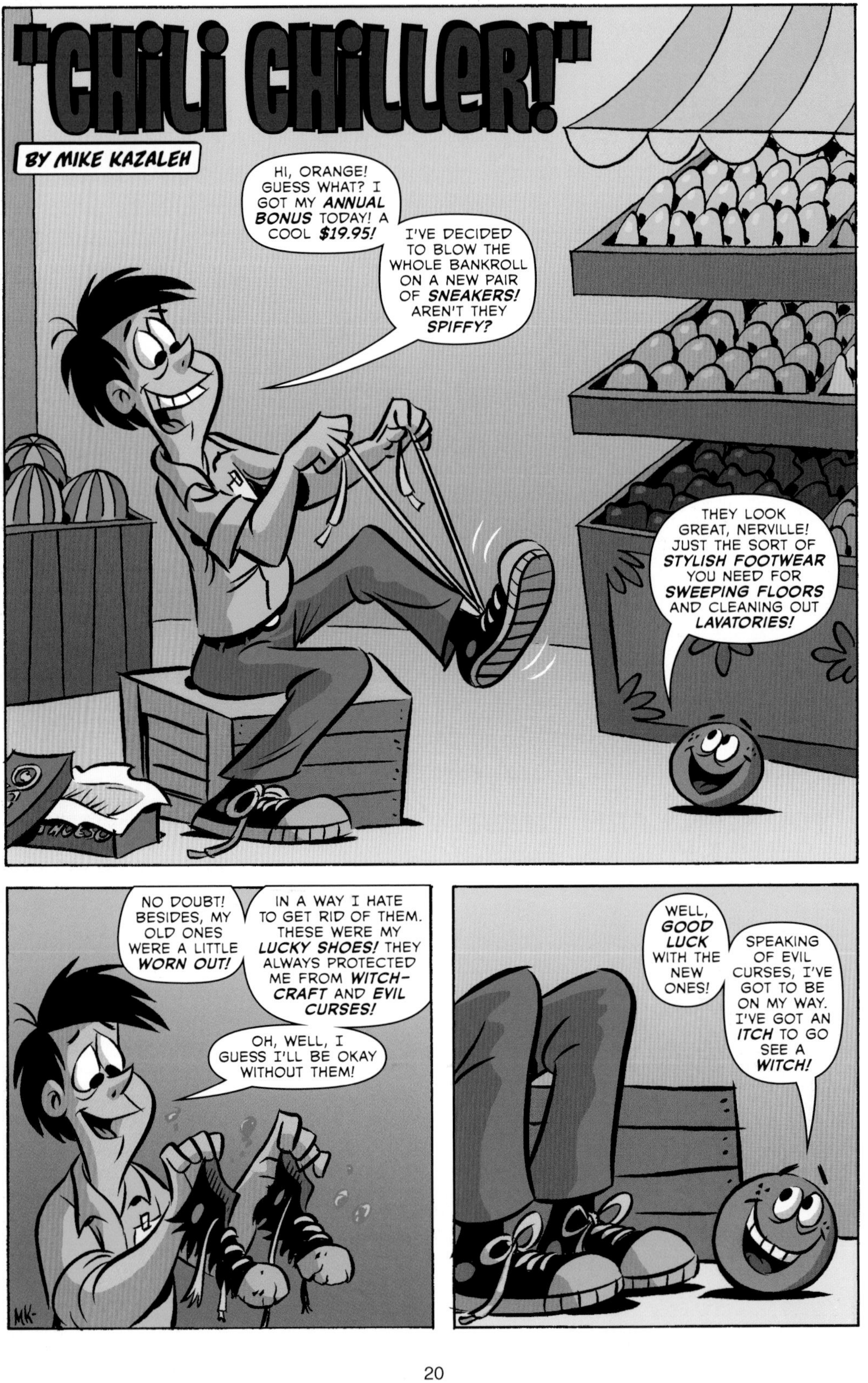

"CHILI CHILLER!"
BY MIKE KAZALEH
HI, ORANGE! GUESS WHAT? I GOT MY ANNUAL BONUS TODAY! A COOL $19.95!
I'VE DECIDED TO BLOW THE WHOLE BANKROLL ON A NEW PAIR OF SNEAKERS! AREN'T THEY SPIFFY?
THEY LOOK GREAT, NERVILLE! JUST THE SORT OF STYLISH FOOTWEAR YOU NEED FOR SWEEPING FLOORS AND CLEANING OUT LAVATORIES!
NO DOUBT! BESIDES, MY OLD ONES WERE A LITTLE WORN OUT!
IN A WAY I HATE TO GET RID OF THEM. THESE WERE MY LUCKY SHOES! THEY ALWAYS PROTECTED ME FROM WITCH-CRAFT AND EVIL CURSES!
OH, WELL, I GUESS I'LL BE OKAY WITHOUT THEM!
WELL, GOOD LUCK WITH THE NEW ONES!
SPEAKING OF EVIL CURSES, I'VE GOT TO BE ON MY WAY. I'VE GOT AN ITCH TO GO SEE A WITCH!

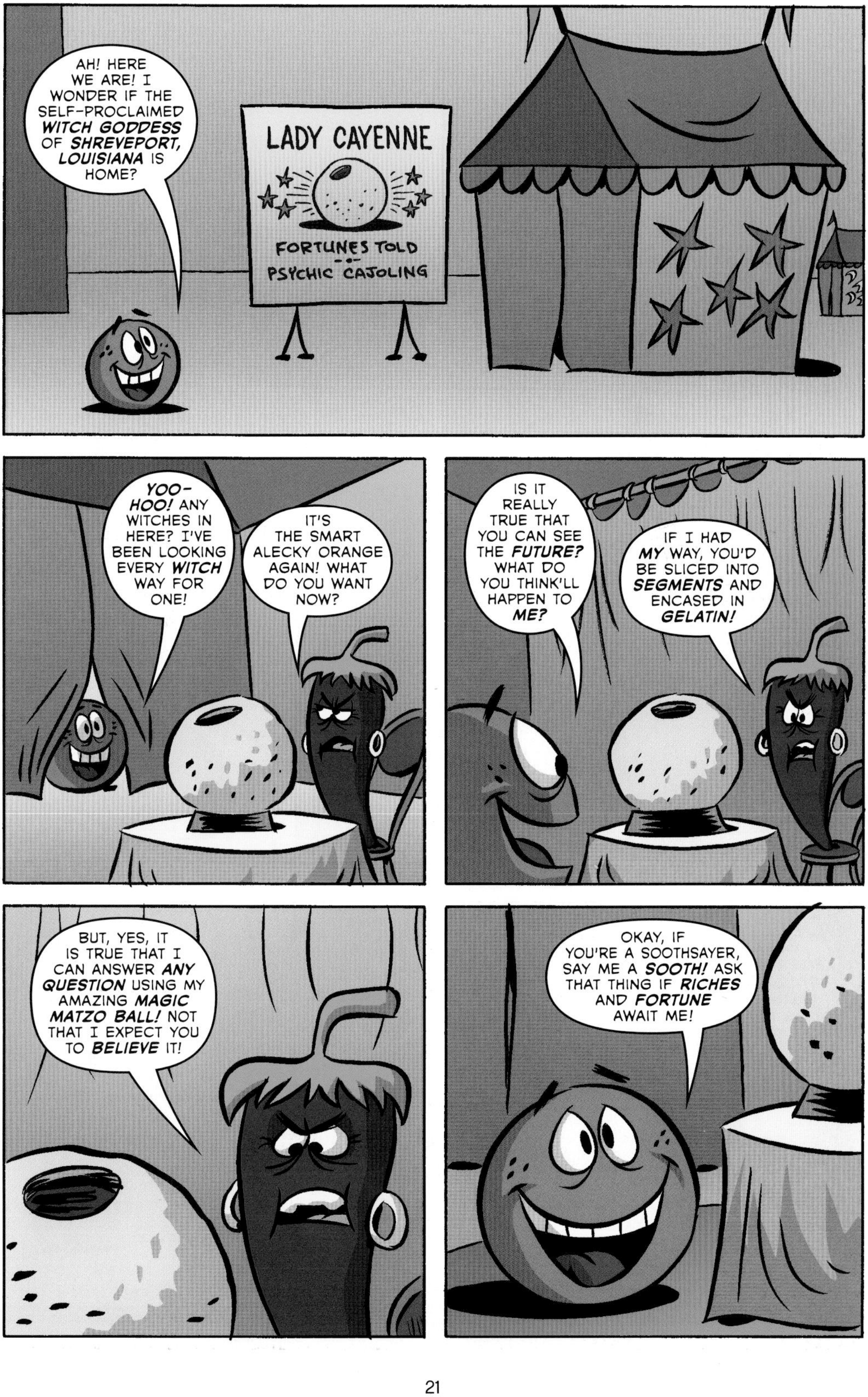
AH! HERE WE ARE! I WONDER IF THE SELF-PROCLAIMED WITCH GODDESS OF SHREVEPORT, LOUISIANA IS HOME?
LADY CAYENNE
FORTUNES TOLD
-o-
PSYCHIC CAJOLING
YOO-HOO! ANY WITCHES IN HERE? I'VE BEEN LOOKING EVERY WITCH WAY FOR ONE!
IT'S THE SMART ALECKY ORANGE AGAIN! WHAT DO YOU WANT NOW?
IS IT REALLY TRUE THAT YOU CAN SEE THE FUTURE? WHAT DO YOU THINK'LL HAPPEN TO ME?
IF I HAD MY WAY, YOU'D BE SLICED INTO SEGMENTS AND ENCASED IN GELATIN!
BUT, YES, IT IS TRUE THAT I CAN ANSWER ANY QUESTION USING MY AMAZING MAGIC MATZO BALL! NOT THAT I EXPECT YOU TO BELIEVE IT!
OKAY, IF YOU'RE A SOOTHSAYER, SAY ME A SOOTH! ASK THAT THING IF RICHES AND FORTUNE AWAIT ME!

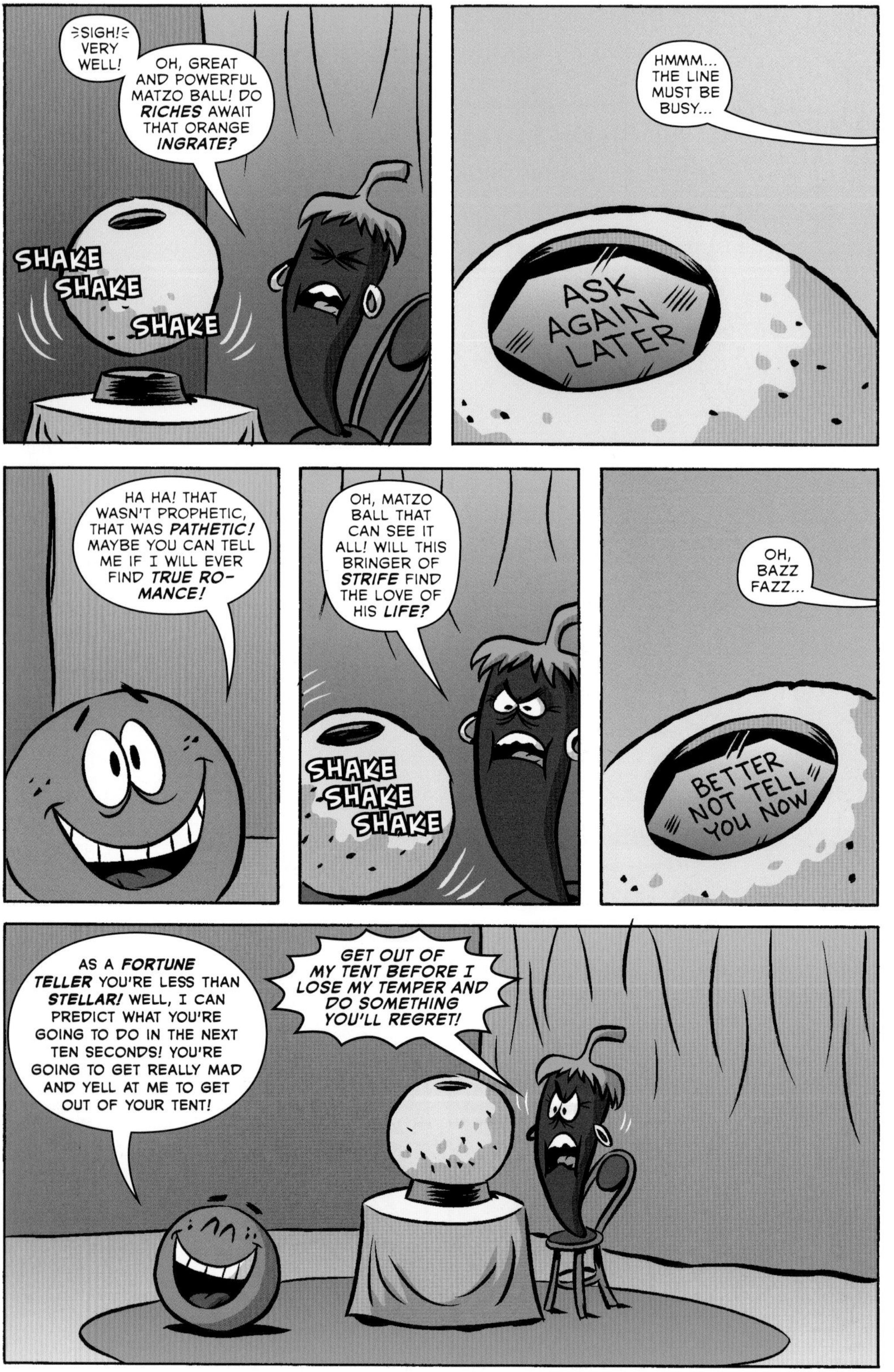
SIGH! VERY WELL!
OH, GREAT AND POWERFUL MATZO BALL! DO RICHES AWAIT THAT ORANGE INGRATE?
SHAKE SHAKE SHAKE
HMMM... THE LINE MUST BE BUSY...
ASK AGAIN LATER
HA HA! THAT WASN'T PROPHETIC, THAT WAS PATHETIC! MAYBE YOU CAN TELL ME IF I WILL EVER FIND TRUE RO-MANCE!
OH, MATZO BALL THAT CAN SEE IT ALL! WILL THIS BRINGER OF STRIFE FIND THE LOVE OF HIS LIFE?
SHAKE SHAKE SHAKE
OH, BAZZ FAZZ...
BETTER NOT TELL YOU NOW
AS A FORTUNE TELLER YOU'RE LESS THAN STELLAR! WELL, I CAN PREDICT WHAT YOU'RE GOING TO DO IN THE NEXT TEN SECONDS! YOU'RE GOING TO GET REALLY MAD AND YELL AT ME TO GET OUT OF YOUR TENT!
GET OUT OF MY TENT BEFORE I LOSE MY TEMPER AND DO SOMETHING YOU'LL REGRET!

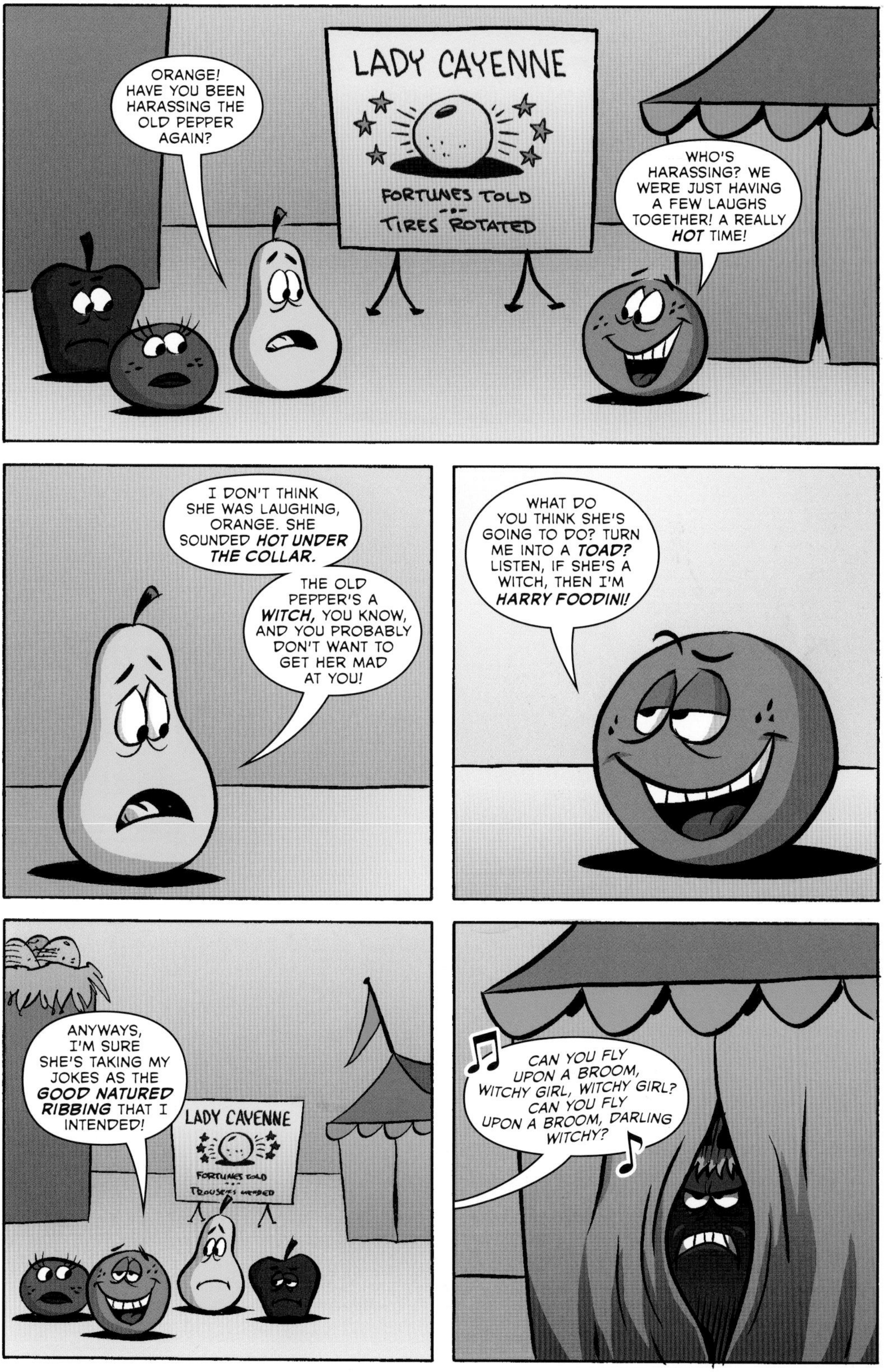
LADY CAYENNE
FORTUNES TOLD
TIRES ROTATED
ORANGE! HAVE YOU BEEN HARASSING THE OLD PEPPER AGAIN?
WHO'S HARASSING? WE WERE JUST HAVING A FEW LAUGHS TOGETHER! A REALLY HOT TIME!
I DON'T THINK SHE WAS LAUGHING, ORANGE. SHE SOUNDED HOT UNDER THE COLLAR.
THE OLD PEPPER'S A WITCH, YOU KNOW, AND YOU PROBABLY DON'T WANT TO GET HER MAD AT YOU!
WHAT DO YOU THINK SHE'S GOING TO DO? TURN ME INTO A TOAD? LISTEN, IF SHE'S A WITCH, THEN I'M HARRY FOODINI!
ANYWAYS, I'M SURE SHE'S TAKING MY JOKES AS THE GOOD NATURED RIBBING THAT I INTENDED!
LADY CAYENNE
FORTUNES TOLD
CAN YOU FLY UPON A BROOM, WITCHY GIRL, WITCHY GIRL? CAN YOU FLY UPON A BROOM, DARLING WITCHY?

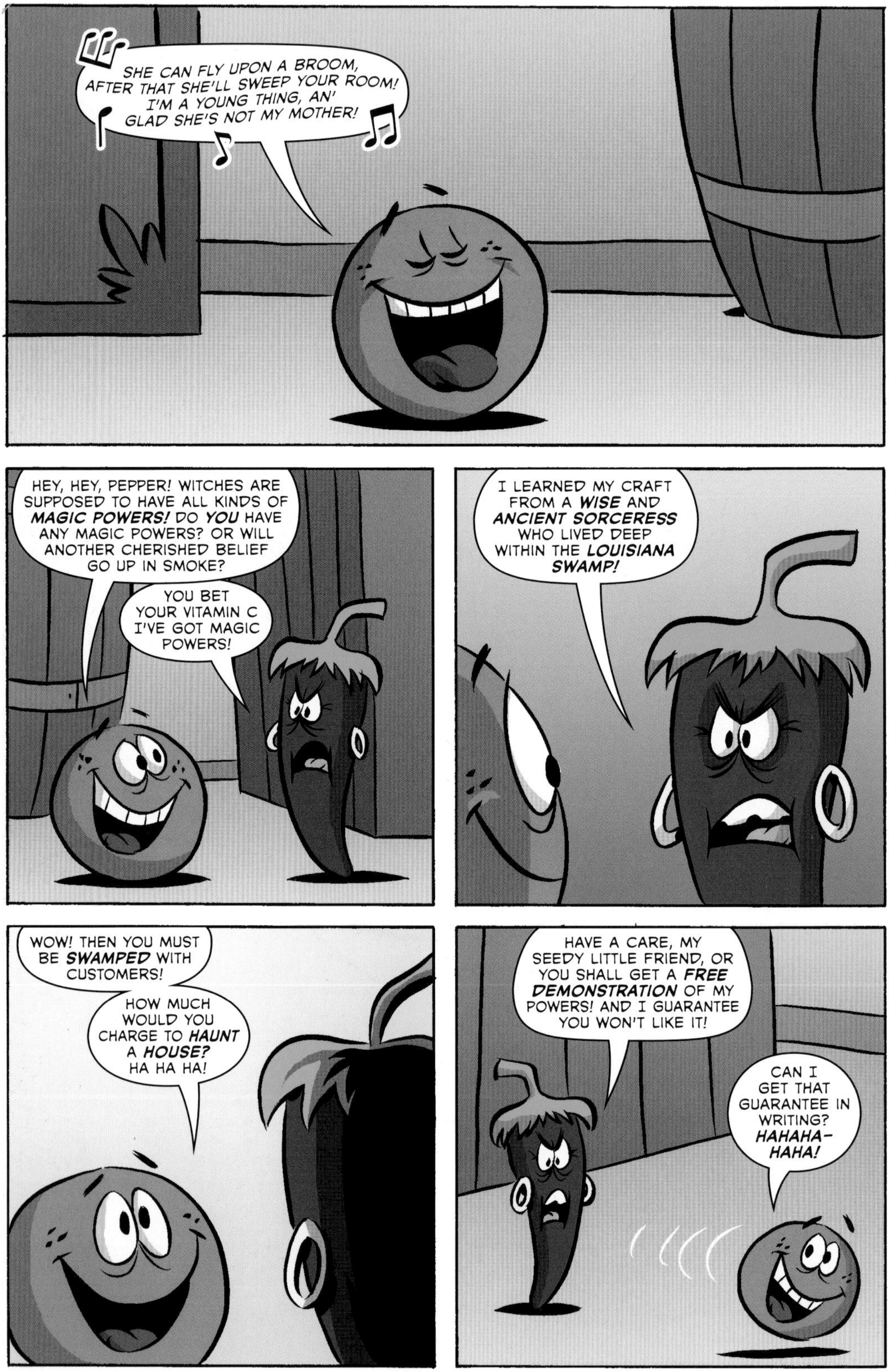
SHE CAN FLY UPON A BROOM, AFTER THAT SHE'LL SWEEP YOUR ROOM! I'M A YOUNG THING, AN' GLAD SHE'S NOT MY MOTHER!
HEY, HEY, PEPPER! WITCHES ARE SUPPOSED TO HAVE ALL KINDS OF MAGIC POWERS! DO YOU HAVE ANY MAGIC POWERS? OR WILL ANOTHER CHERISHED BELIEF GO UP IN SMOKE?
YOU BET YOUR VITAMIN C I'VE GOT MAGIC POWERS!
I LEARNED MY CRAFT FROM A WISE AND ANCIENT SORCERESS WHO LIVED DEEP WITHIN THE LOUISIANA SWAMP!
WOW! THEN YOU MUST BE SWAMPED WITH CUSTOMERS!
HOW MUCH WOULD YOU CHARGE TO HAUNT A HOUSE? HA HA HA!
HAVE A CARE, MY SEEDY LITTLE FRIEND, OR YOU SHALL GET A FREE DEMONSTRATION OF MY POWERS! AND I GUARANTEE YOU WON'T LIKE IT!
CAN I GET THAT GUARANTEE IN WRITING? HAHAHA-HAHA!

MORNING AGAIN... ONE MORE DAY OF BEING THE BUTT OF THAT SILLY CITRUS' JOKES...

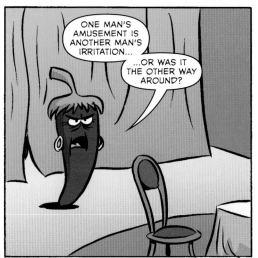

ONE MAN'S AMUSEMENT IS ANOTHER MAN'S IRRITATION...

...OR WAS IT THE OTHER WAY AROUND?

HEY! WHAT IN THE BLINKIN' BLUE BLAZES...?

MY MAGIC MATZO BALL! IT'S *GONE!*

SOMEBODY TOOK IT AND I THINK I KNOW *WHO!*

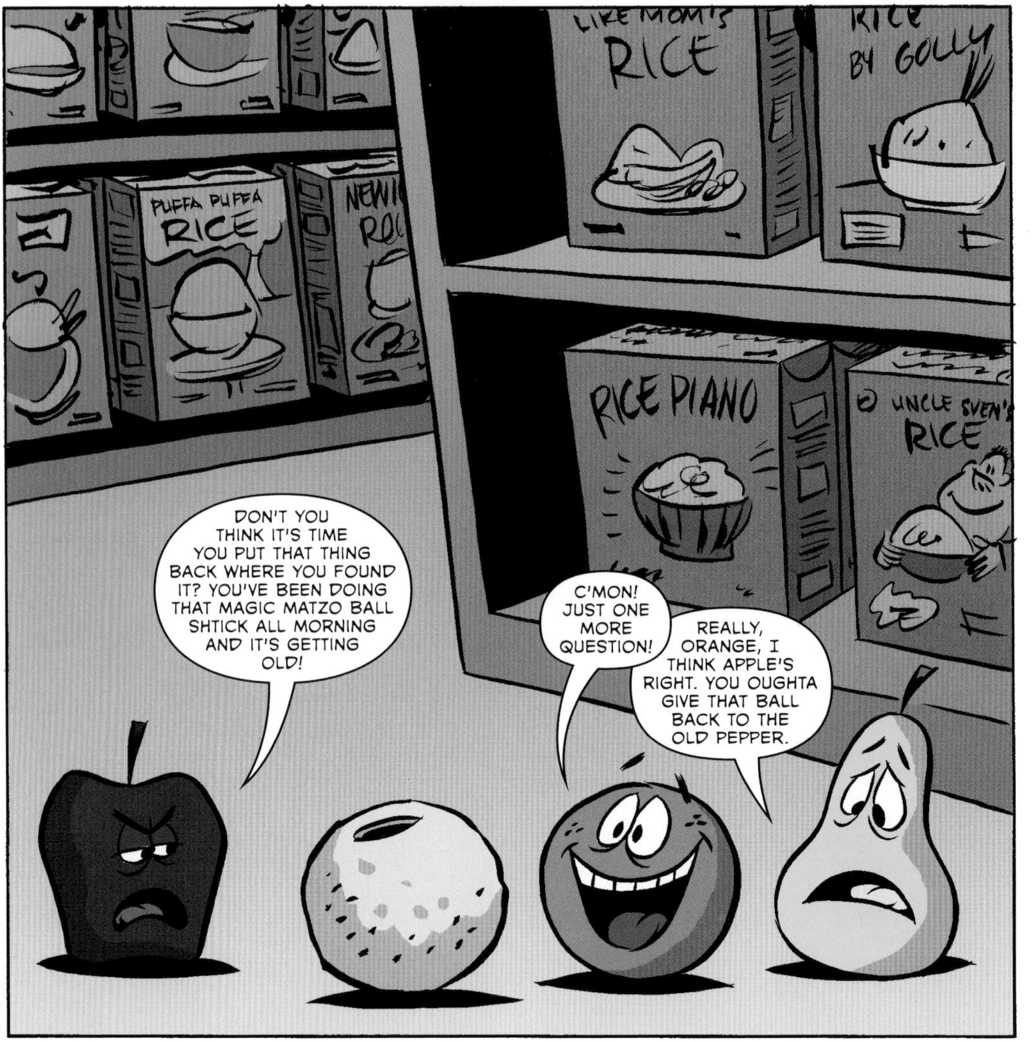
LIKE MOM'S RICE
RICE BY GOLLY
PUFFA PUFFA RICE
RICE PIANO
UNCLE SVEN'S RICE
DON'T YOU THINK IT'S TIME YOU PUT THAT THING BACK WHERE YOU FOUND IT? YOU'VE BEEN DOING THAT MAGIC MATZO BALL SHTICK ALL MORNING AND IT'S GETTING OLD!
C'MON! JUST ONE MORE QUESTION!
REALLY, ORANGE, I THINK APPLE'S RIGHT. YOU OUGHTA GIVE THAT BALL BACK TO THE OLD PEPPER.

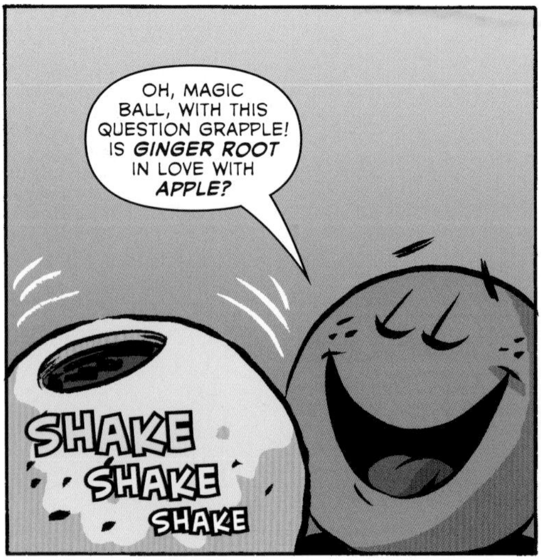
OH, MAGIC BALL, WITH THIS QUESTION GRAPPLE! IS ***GINGER ROOT*** IN LOVE WITH ***APPLE?***
SHAKE SHAKE SHAKE

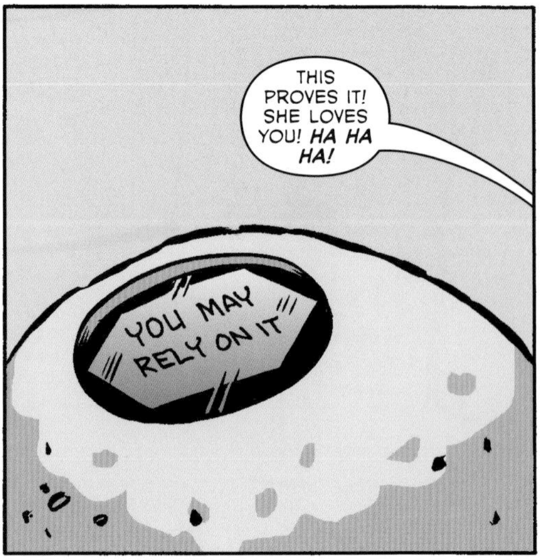
THIS PROVES IT! SHE LOVES YOU! ***HA HA HA!***
YOU MAY RELY ON IT

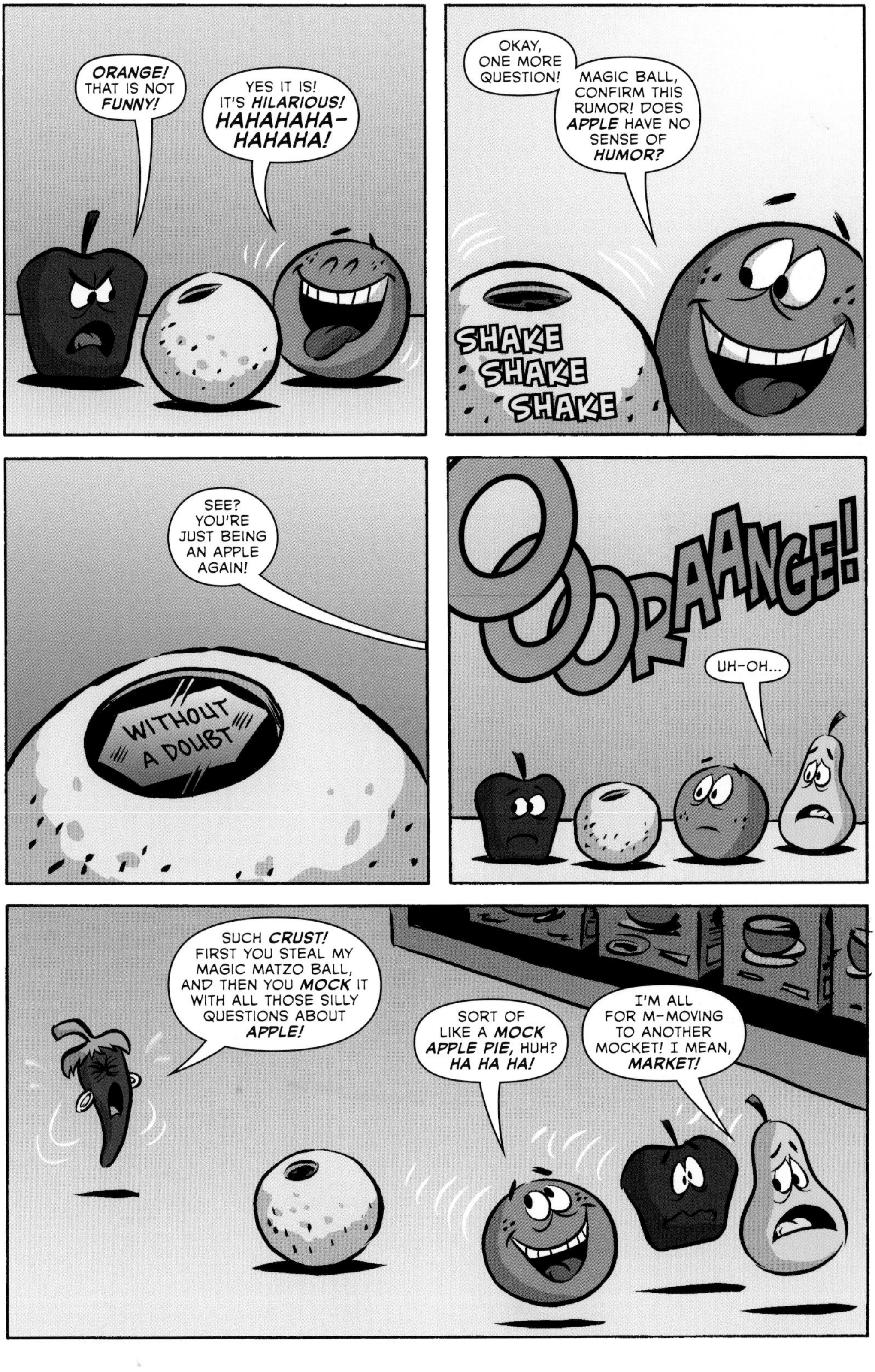
ORANGE! THAT IS NOT FUNNY!
YES IT IS! IT'S HILARIOUS! HAHAHAHA-HAHAHA!
OKAY, ONE MORE QUESTION!
MAGIC BALL, CONFIRM THIS RUMOR! DOES APPLE HAVE NO SENSE OF HUMOR?
SHAKE SHAKE SHAKE
SEE? YOU'RE JUST BEING AN APPLE AGAIN!
WITHOUT A DOUBT
OORAANGE!
UH-OH...
SUCH CRUST! FIRST YOU STEAL MY MAGIC MATZO BALL, AND THEN YOU MOCK IT WITH ALL THOSE SILLY QUESTIONS ABOUT APPLE!
SORT OF LIKE A MOCK APPLE PIE, HUH? HA HA HA!
I'M ALL FOR M-MOVING TO ANOTHER MOCKET! I MEAN, MARKET!

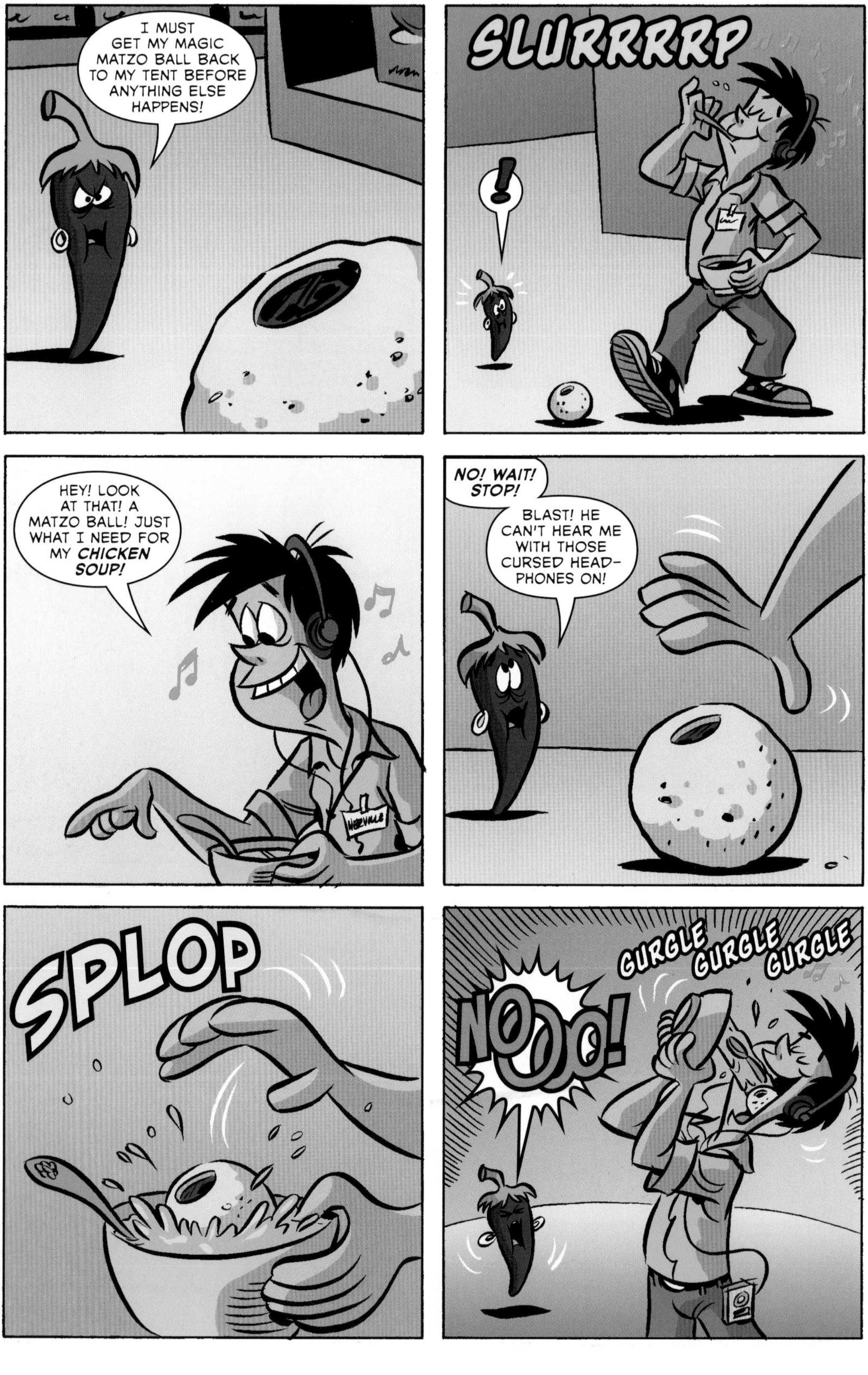
I MUST GET MY MAGIC MATZO BALL BACK TO MY TENT BEFORE ANYTHING ELSE HAPPENS!
SLURRRRRP
!
HEY! LOOK AT THAT! A MATZO BALL! JUST WHAT I NEED FOR MY CHICKEN SOUP!
NO! WAIT! STOP!
BLAST! HE CAN'T HEAR ME WITH THOSE CURSED HEAD-PHONES ON!
SPLOP
GURGLE GURGLE GURGLE
NOOOO!

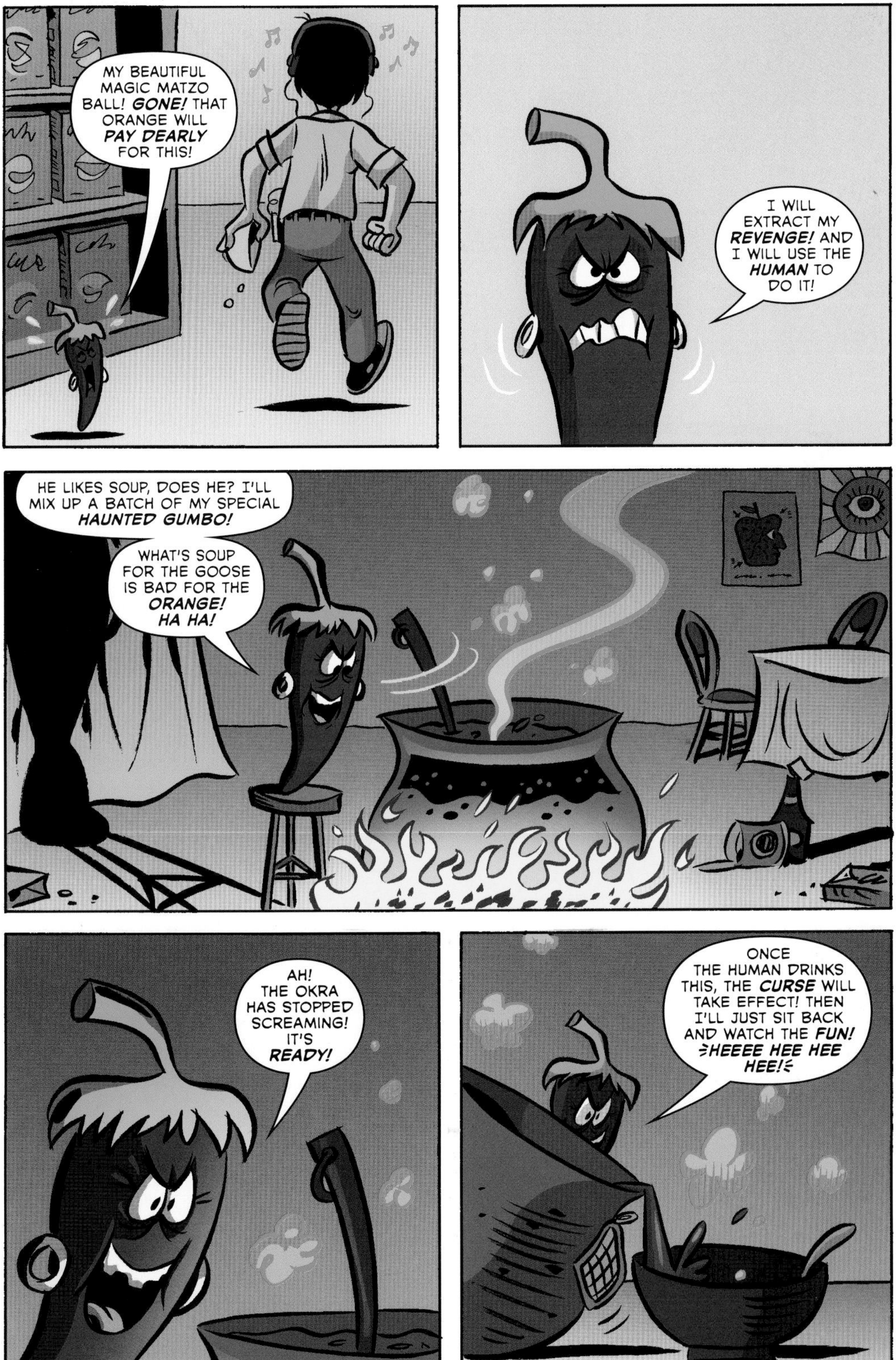
MY BEAUTIFUL MAGIC MATZO BALL! GONE! THAT ORANGE WILL PAY DEARLY FOR THIS!
I WILL EXTRACT MY REVENGE! AND I WILL USE THE HUMAN TO DO IT!
HE LIKES SOUP, DOES HE? I'LL MIX UP A BATCH OF MY SPECIAL HAUNTED GUMBO!
WHAT'S SOUP FOR THE GOOSE IS BAD FOR THE ORANGE! HA HA!
AH! THE OKRA HAS STOPPED SCREAMING! IT'S READY!
ONCE THE HUMAN DRINKS THIS, THE CURSE WILL TAKE EFFECT! THEN I'LL JUST SIT BACK AND WATCH THE FUN! HEEEE HEE HEE HEE!

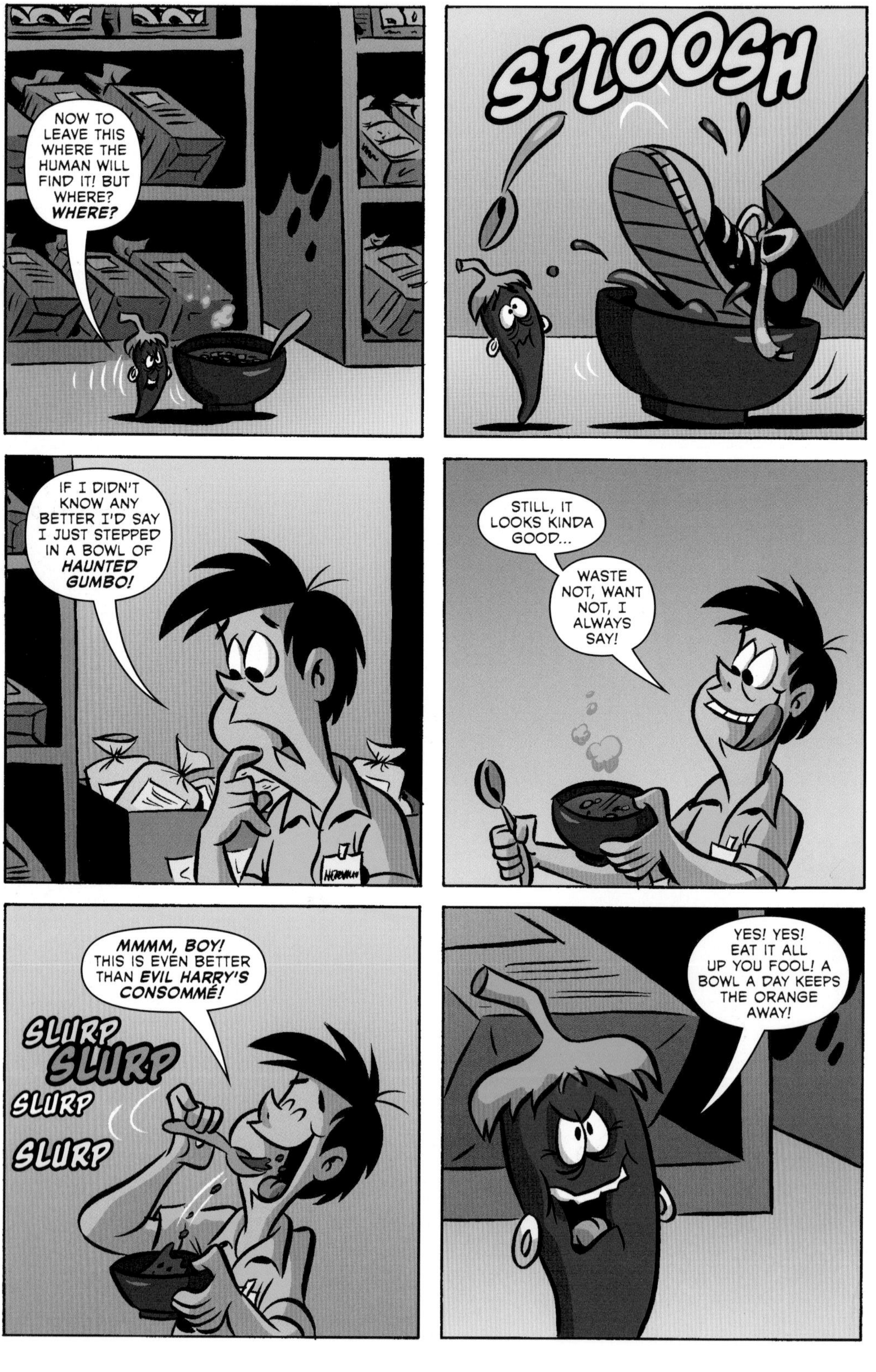
NOW TO LEAVE THIS WHERE THE HUMAN WILL FIND IT! BUT WHERE? WHERE?
SPLOOSH
IF I DIDN'T KNOW ANY BETTER I'D SAY I JUST STEPPED IN A BOWL OF HAUNTED GUMBO!
STILL, IT LOOKS KINDA GOOD...
WASTE NOT, WANT NOT, I ALWAYS SAY!
MMMM, BOY! THIS IS EVEN BETTER THAN EVIL HARRY'S CONSOMMÉ!
SLURP
SLURP
SLURP
SLURP
YES! YES! EAT IT ALL UP YOU FOOL! A BOWL A DAY KEEPS THE ORANGE AWAY!

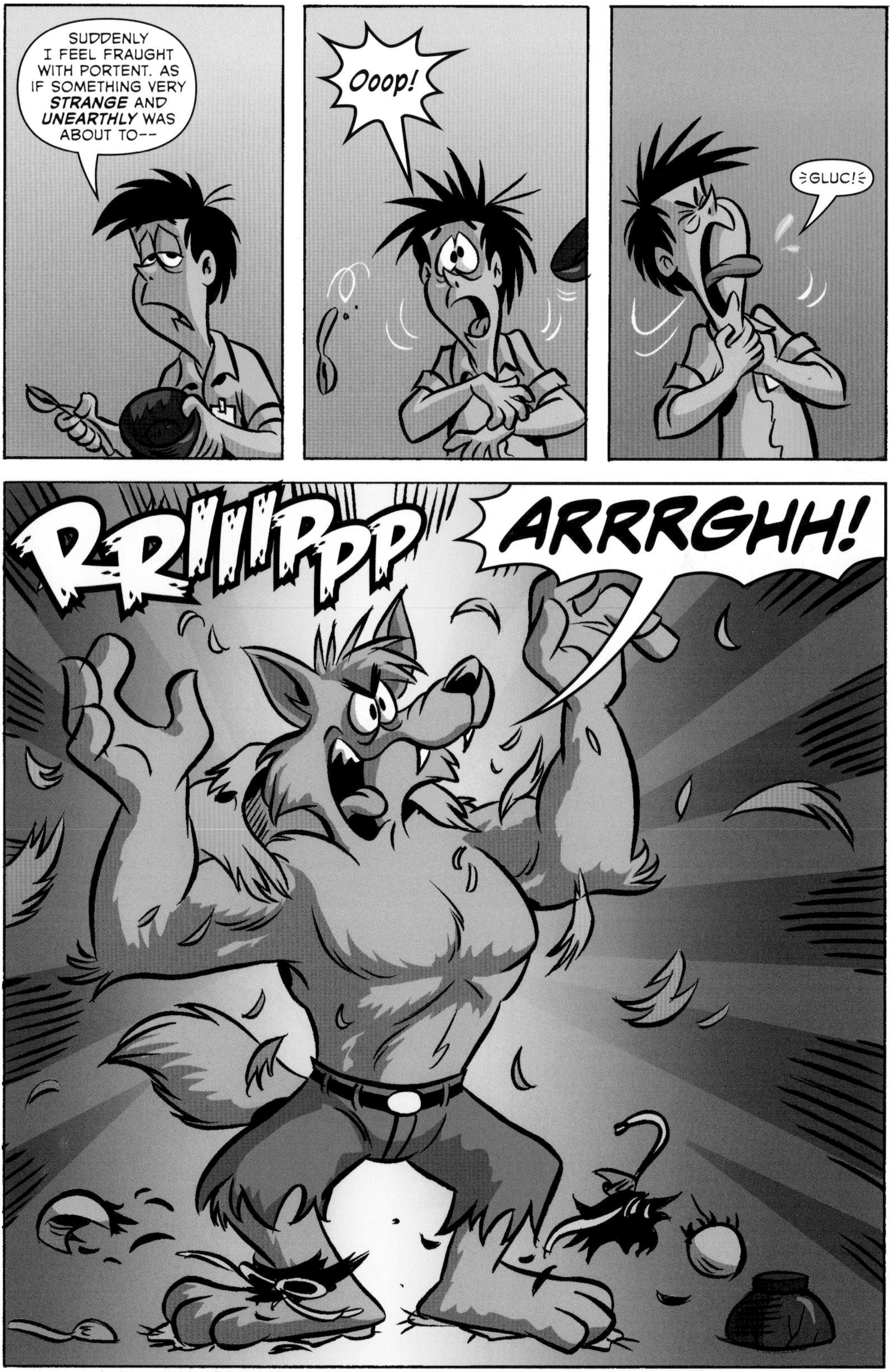
SUDDENLY I FEEL FRAUGHT WITH PORTENT. AS IF SOMETHING VERY STRANGE AND UNEARTHLY WAS ABOUT TO--
Ooop!
GLUC!
RRIIIPPP
ARRRGHH!

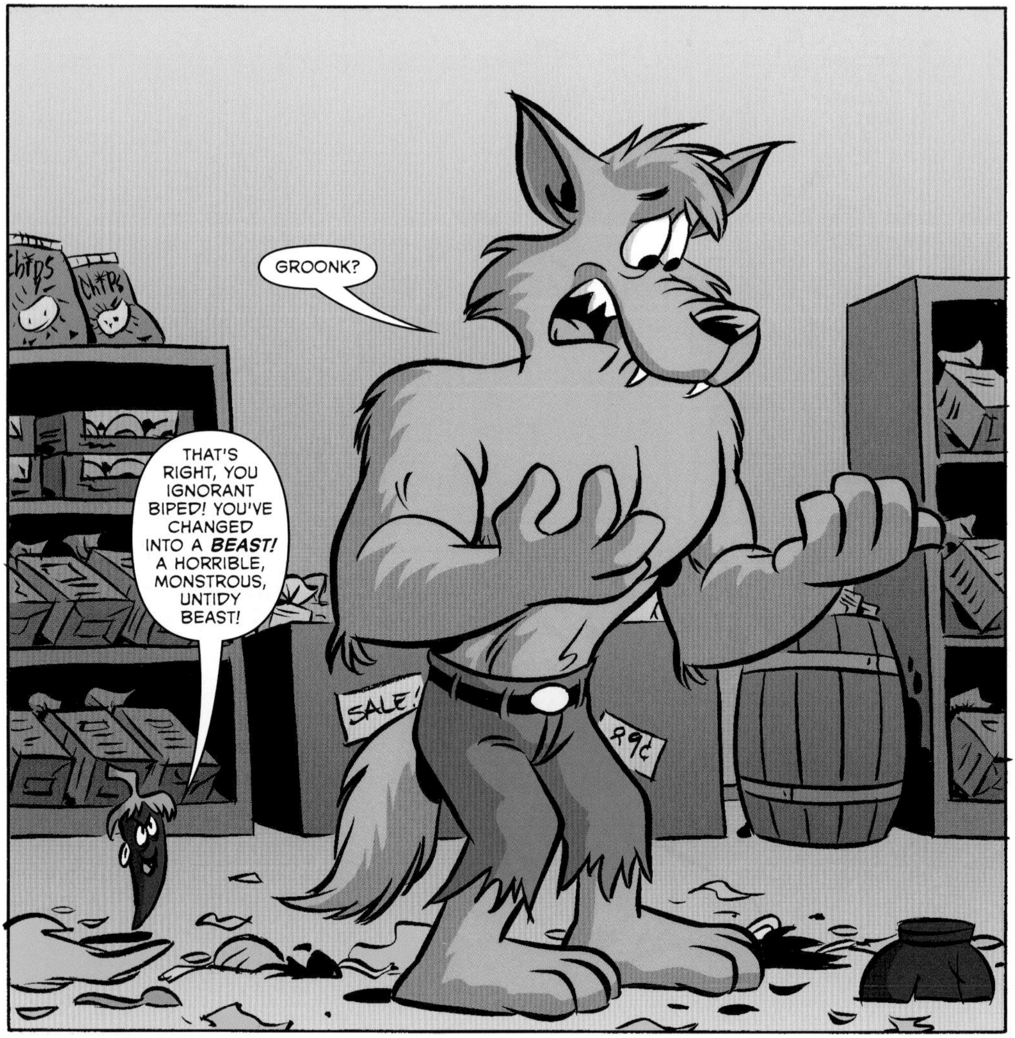
GROONK?
THAT'S RIGHT, YOU IGNORANT BIPED! YOU'VE CHANGED INTO A ***BEAST!*** A HORRIBLE, MONSTROUS, UNTIDY BEAST!
SALE!
99¢

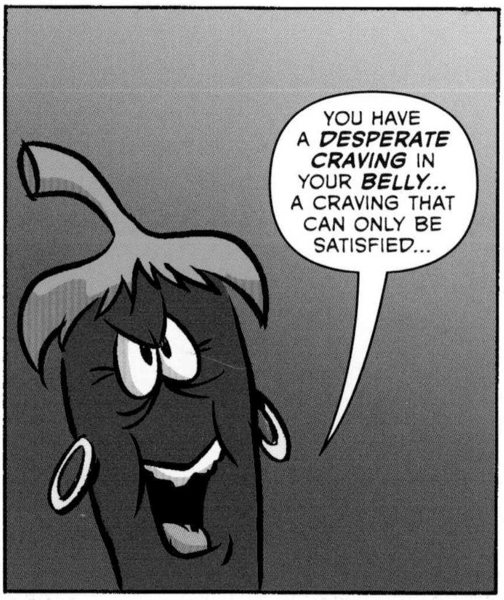
YOU HAVE A ***DESPERATE CRAVING*** IN YOUR ***BELLY...*** A CRAVING THAT CAN ONLY BE SATISFIED...

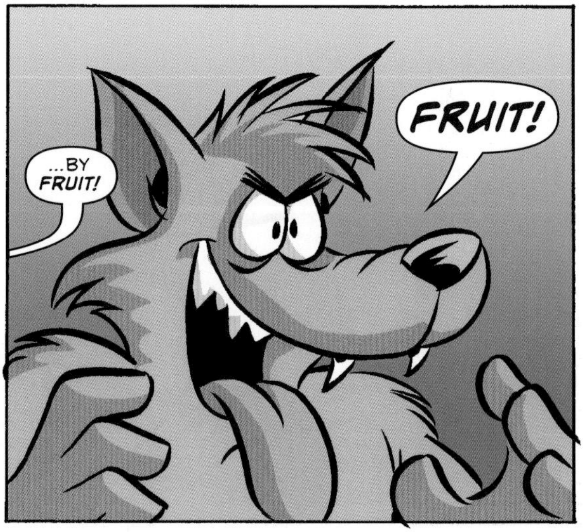
...BY ***FRUIT!***
FRUIT!

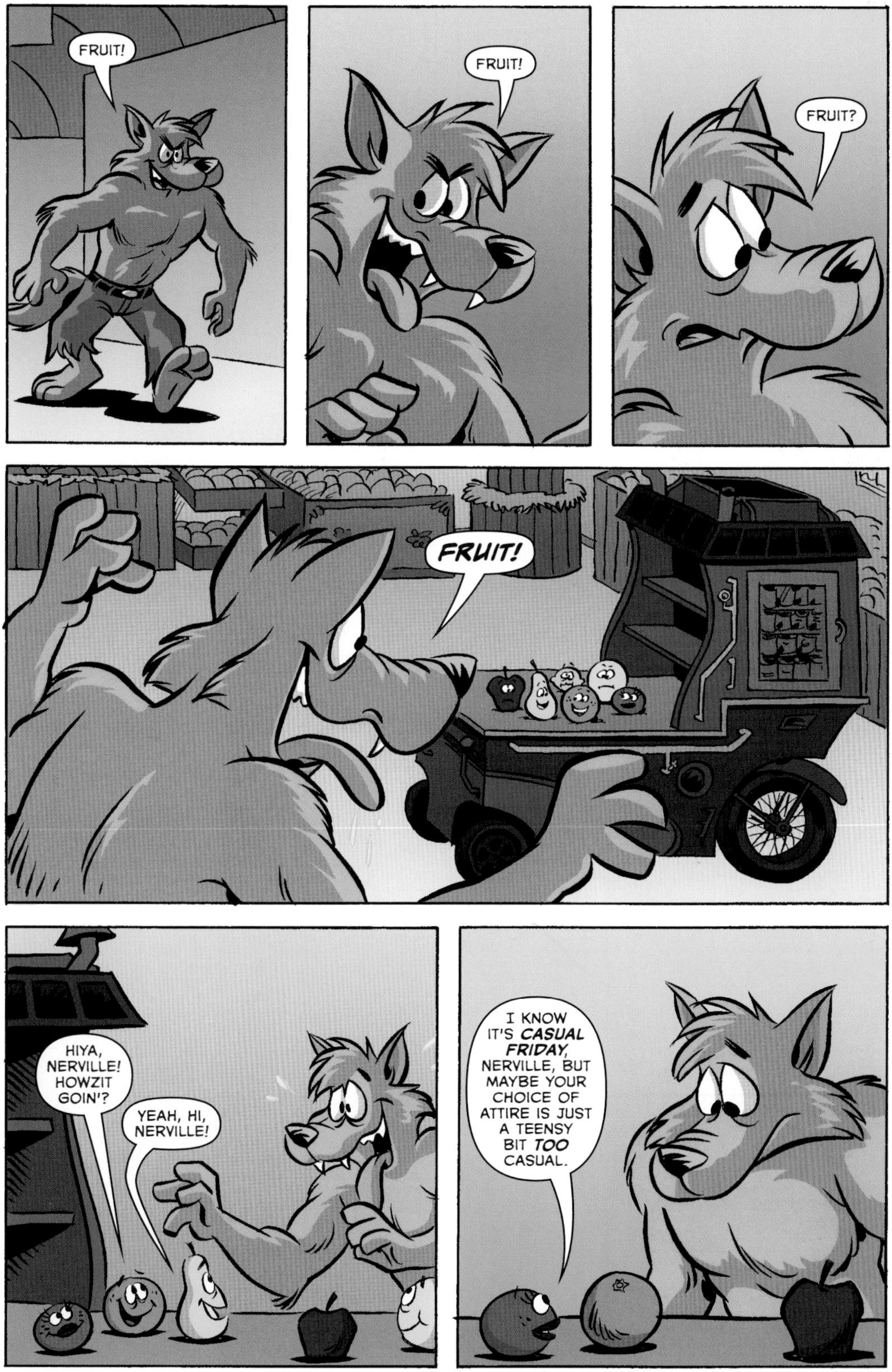
FRUIT!
FRUIT!
FRUIT?
FRUIT!
HIYA, NERVILLE! HOWZIT GOIN'?
YEAH, HI, NERVILLE!
I KNOW IT'S *CASUAL FRIDAY*, NERVILLE, BUT MAYBE YOUR CHOICE OF ATTIRE IS JUST A TEENSY BIT *TOO* CASUAL.

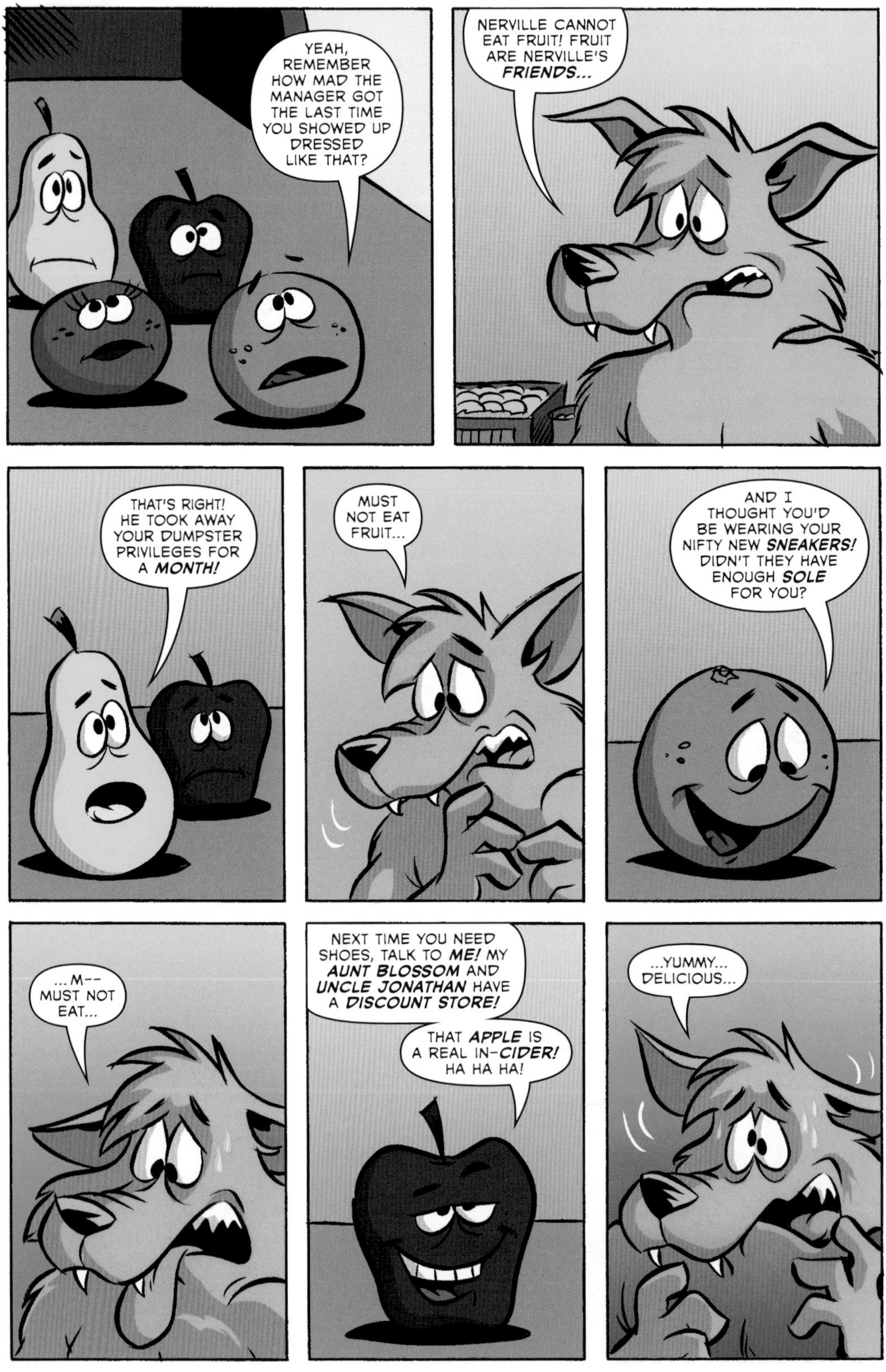
YEAH, REMEMBER HOW MAD THE MANAGER GOT THE LAST TIME YOU SHOWED UP DRESSED LIKE THAT?
NERVILLE CANNOT EAT FRUIT! FRUIT ARE NERVILLE'S FRIENDS...
THAT'S RIGHT! HE TOOK AWAY YOUR DUMPSTER PRIVILEGES FOR A MONTH!
MUST NOT EAT FRUIT...
AND I THOUGHT YOU'D BE WEARING YOUR NIFTY NEW SNEAKERS! DIDN'T THEY HAVE ENOUGH SOLE FOR YOU?
...M-- MUST NOT EAT...
NEXT TIME YOU NEED SHOES, TALK TO ME! MY AUNT BLOSSOM AND UNCLE JONATHAN HAVE A DISCOUNT STORE!
THAT APPLE IS A REAL IN-CIDER! HA HA HA!
...YUMMY... DELICIOUS...

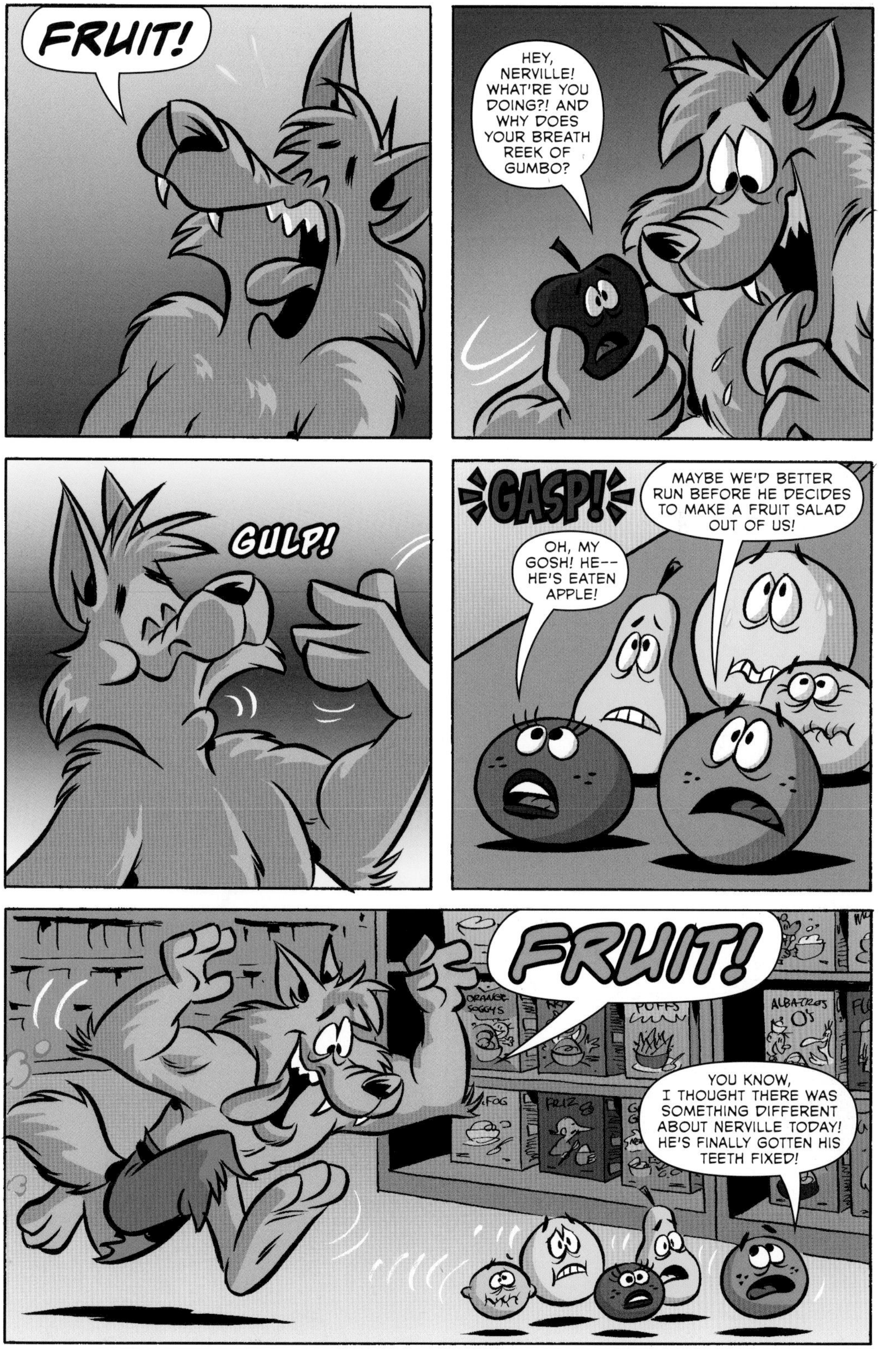
FRUIT!
HEY, NERVILLE! WHAT'RE YOU DOING?! AND WHY DOES YOUR BREATH REEK OF GUMBO?
GULP!
GASP!
MAYBE WE'D BETTER RUN BEFORE HE DECIDES TO MAKE A FRUIT SALAD OUT OF US!
OH, MY GOSH! HE-- HE'S EATEN APPLE!
FRUIT!
YOU KNOW, I THOUGHT THERE WAS SOMETHING DIFFERENT ABOUT NERVILLE TODAY! HE'S FINALLY GOTTEN HIS TEETH FIXED!

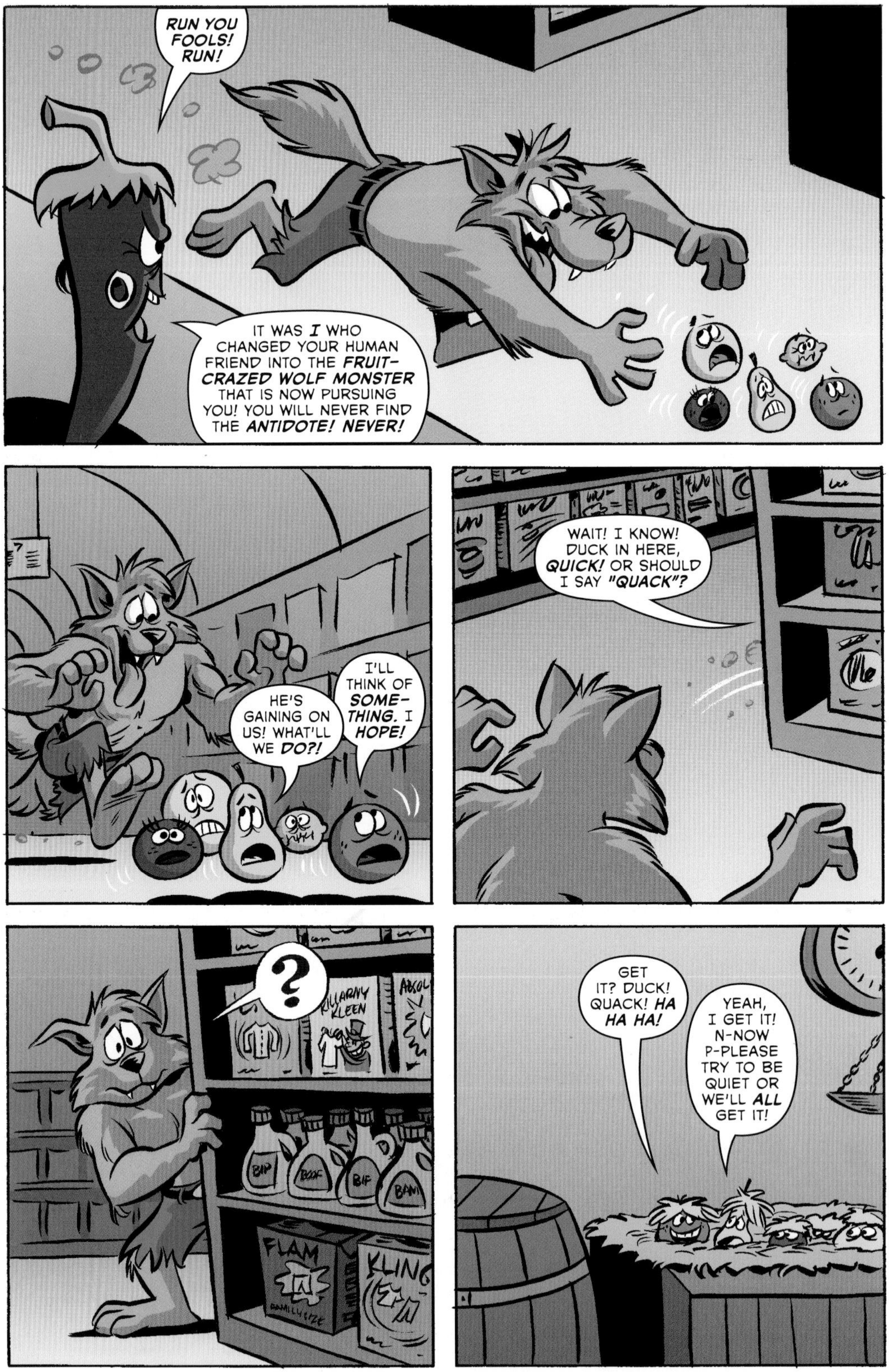

RUN YOU FOOLS! RUN!
IT WAS *I* WHO CHANGED YOUR HUMAN FRIEND INTO THE ***FRUIT-CRAZED WOLF MONSTER*** THAT IS NOW PURSUING YOU! YOU WILL NEVER FIND THE ***ANTIDOTE! NEVER!***
HE'S GAINING ON US! WHAT'LL WE ***DO?!***
I'LL THINK OF ***SOME-THING.*** I ***HOPE!***
WAIT! I KNOW! DUCK IN HERE, ***QUICK!*** OR SHOULD I SAY ***"QUACK"?***
?
KILLARNY KLEEN
FLAM
KLING
GET IT? DUCK! QUACK! ***HA HA HA!***
YEAH, I GET IT! N-NOW P-PLEASE TRY TO BE QUIET OR WE'LL ***ALL*** GET IT!

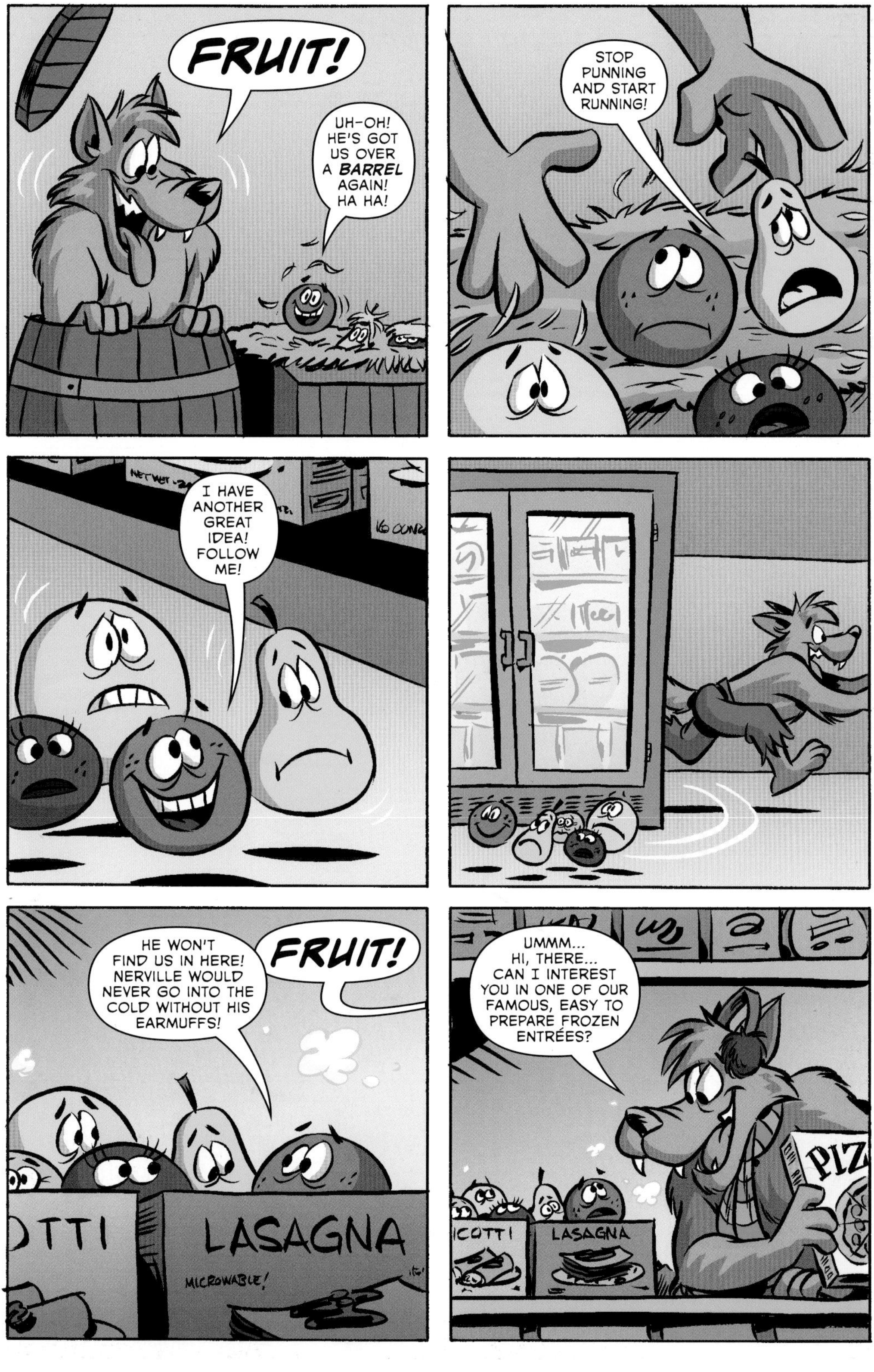
FRUIT!
UH-OH! HE'S GOT US OVER A BARREL AGAIN! HA HA!
STOP PUNNING AND START RUNNING!
I HAVE ANOTHER GREAT IDEA! FOLLOW ME!
HE WON'T FIND US IN HERE! NERVILLE WOULD NEVER GO INTO THE COLD WITHOUT HIS EARMUFFS!
FRUIT!
OTTI
LASAGNA
MICROWABLE!
UMMM... HI, THERE... CAN I INTEREST YOU IN ONE OF OUR FAMOUS, EASY TO PREPARE FROZEN ENTRÉES?
ICOTTI
LASAGNA
PIZ

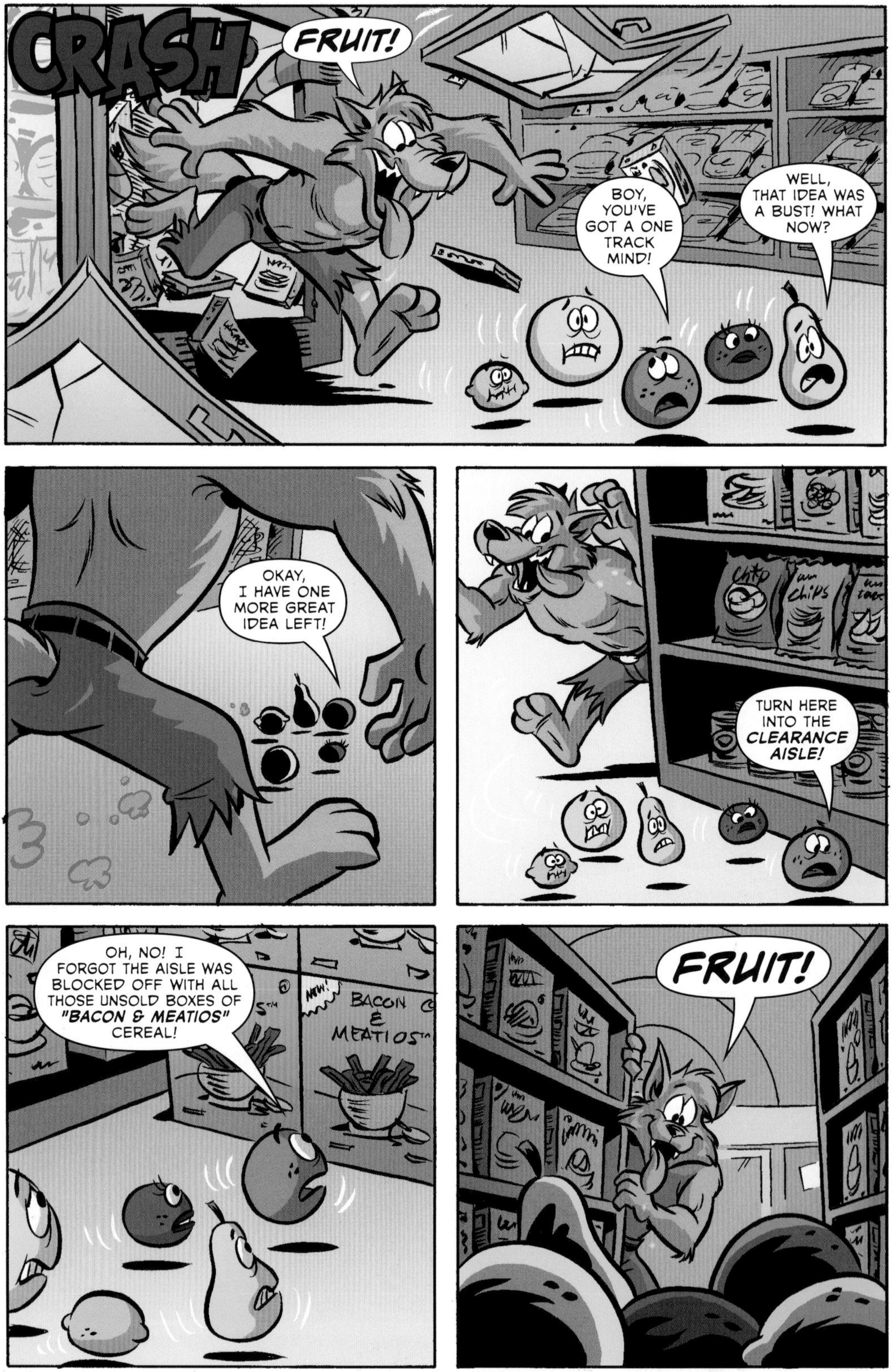
CRASH
FRUIT!
BOY, YOU'VE GOT A ONE TRACK MIND!
WELL, THAT IDEA WAS A BUST! WHAT NOW?
OKAY, I HAVE ONE MORE GREAT IDEA LEFT!
TURN HERE INTO THE CLEARANCE AISLE!
OH, NO! I FORGOT THE AISLE WAS BLOCKED OFF WITH ALL THOSE UNSOLD BOXES OF "BACON & MEATIOS" CEREAL!
BACON & MEATIOS™
FRUIT!

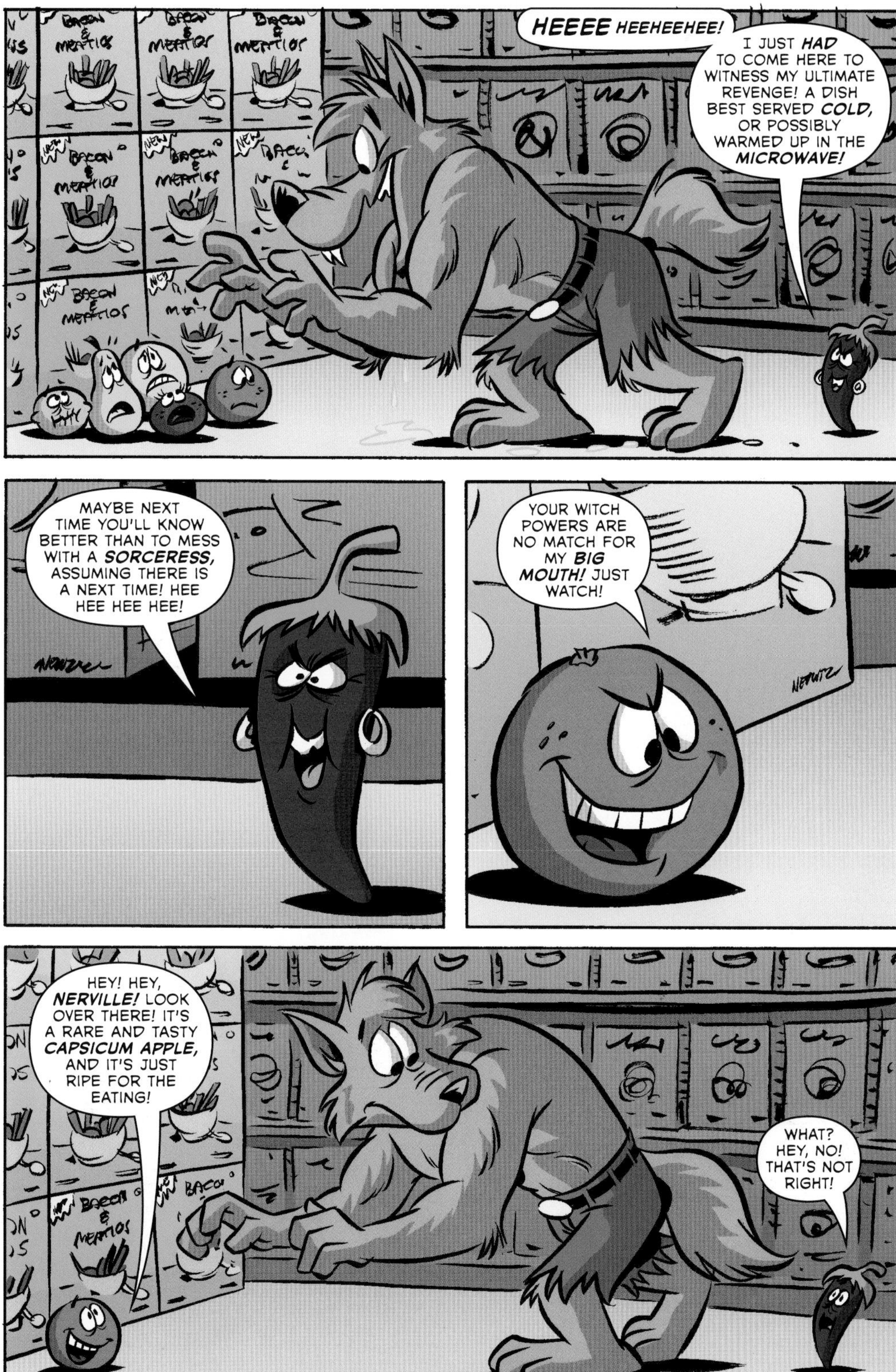
HEEEE HEEHEEHEE!
I JUST HAD TO COME HERE TO WITNESS MY ULTIMATE REVENGE! A DISH BEST SERVED COLD, OR POSSIBLY WARMED UP IN THE MICROWAVE!
MAYBE NEXT TIME YOU'LL KNOW BETTER THAN TO MESS WITH A SORCERESS, ASSUMING THERE IS A NEXT TIME! HEE HEE HEE HEE!
YOUR WITCH POWERS ARE NO MATCH FOR MY BIG MOUTH! JUST WATCH!
HEY! HEY, NERVILLE! LOOK OVER THERE! IT'S A RARE AND TASTY CAPSICUM APPLE, AND IT'S JUST RIPE FOR THE EATING!
WHAT? HEY, NO! THAT'S NOT RIGHT!

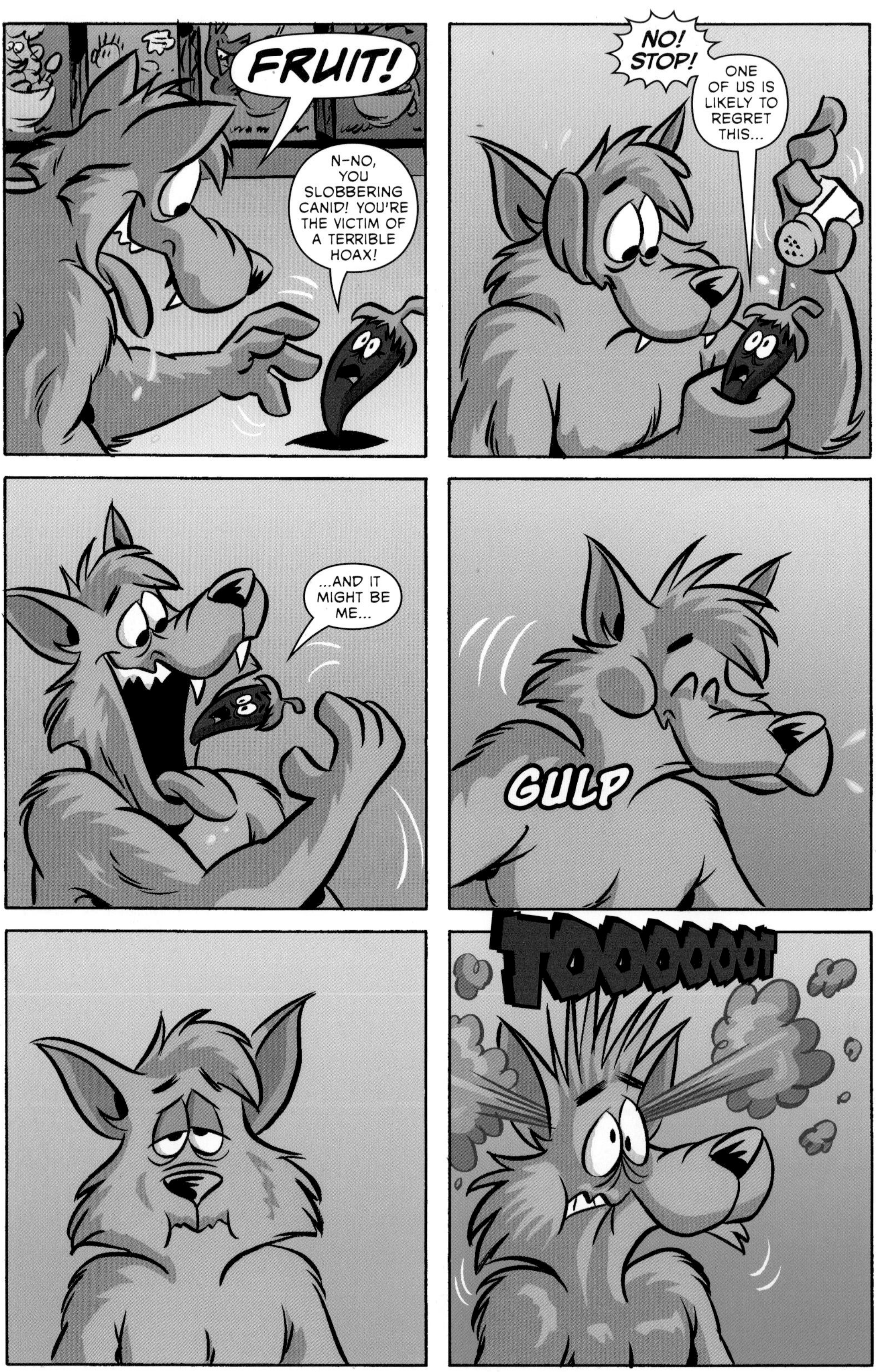
FRUIT!
N-NO, YOU SLOBBERING CANID! YOU'RE THE VICTIM OF A TERRIBLE HOAX!
NO! STOP!
ONE OF US IS LIKELY TO REGRET THIS...
...AND IT MIGHT BE ME...
GULP
TOOOOOOT

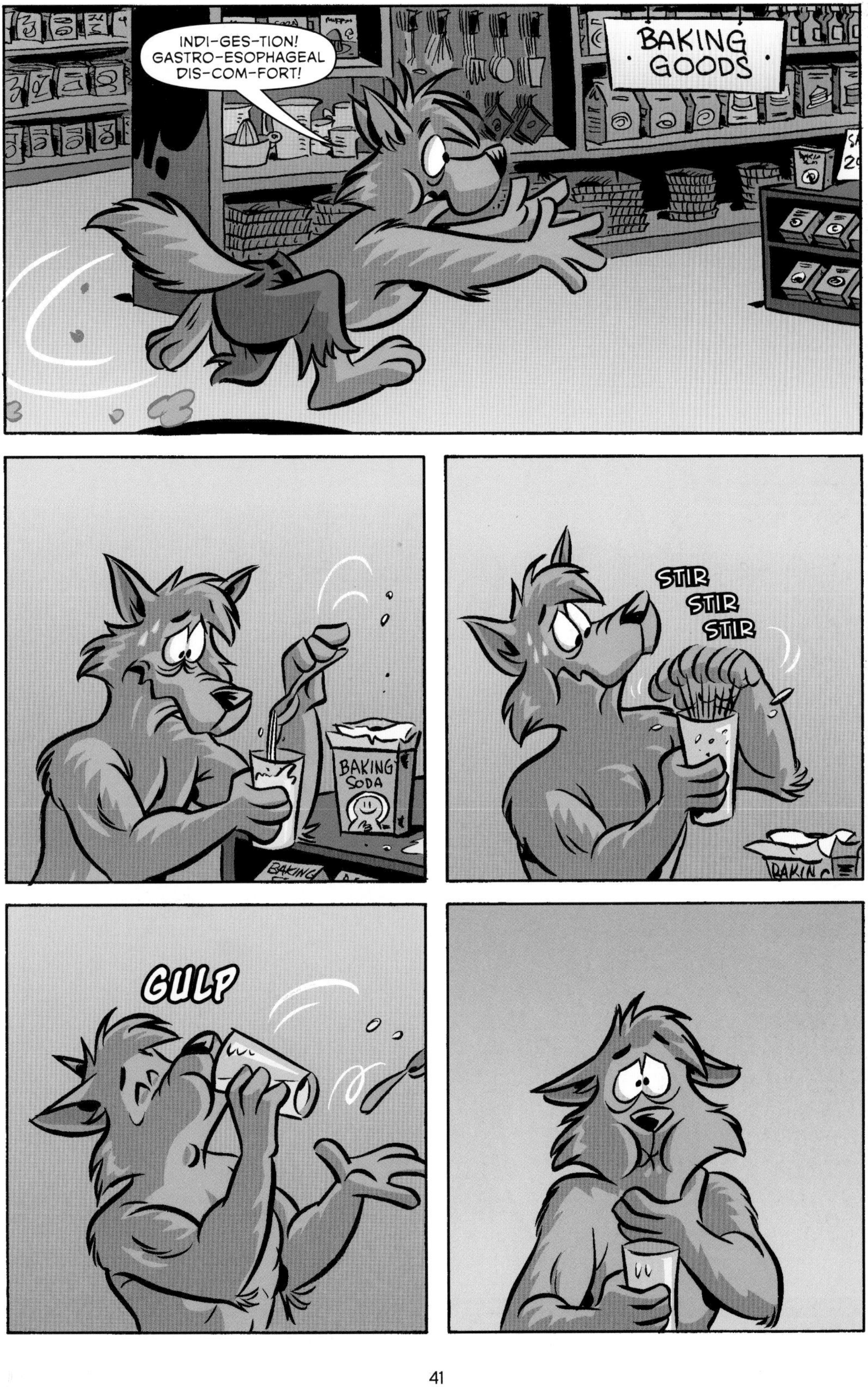
INDI-GES-TION! GASTRO-ESOPHAGEAL DIS-COM-FORT!
BAKING GOODS
BAKING SODA
STIR
STIR
STIR
GULP

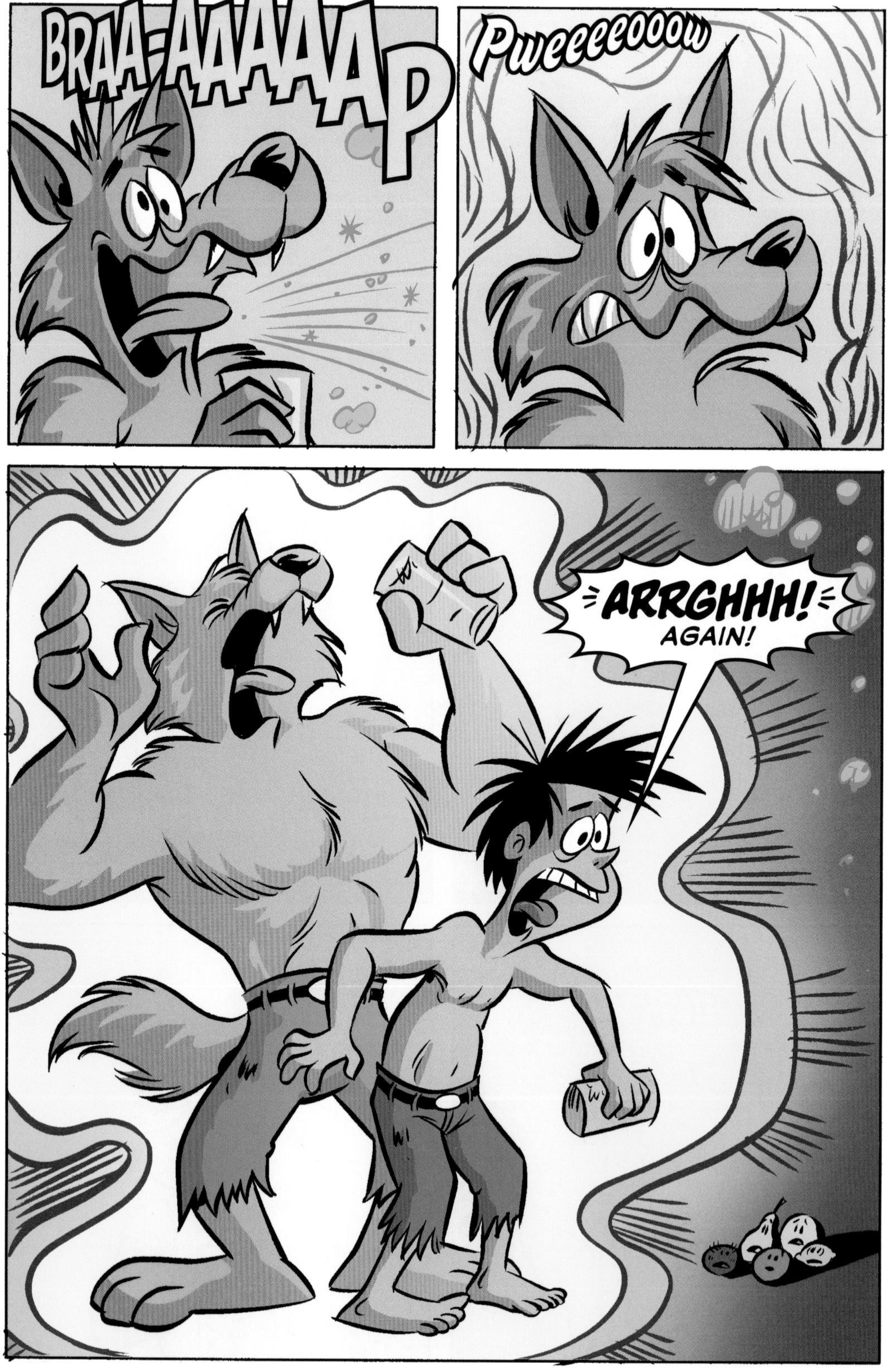
BRAA-AAAAAP
Pweeeeooow
ARRGHHH!
AGAIN!

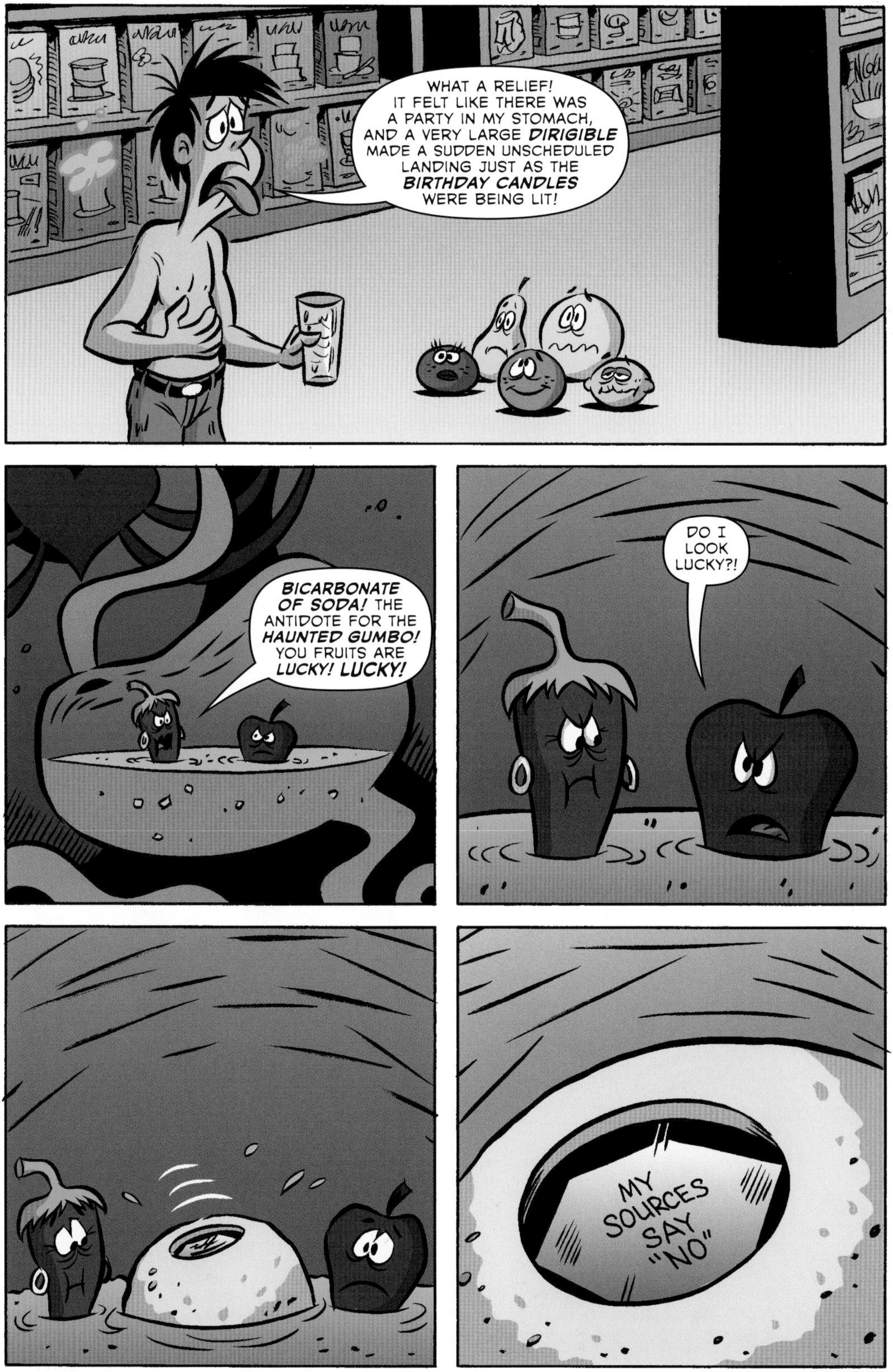
WHAT A RELIEF! IT FELT LIKE THERE WAS A PARTY IN MY STOMACH, AND A VERY LARGE DIRIGIBLE MADE A SUDDEN UNSCHEDULED LANDING JUST AS THE BIRTHDAY CANDLES WERE BEING LIT!
BICARBONATE OF SODA! THE ANTIDOTE FOR THE HAUNTED GUMBO! YOU FRUITS ARE LUCKY! LUCKY!
DO I LOOK LUCKY?!
MY SOURCES SAY "NO"

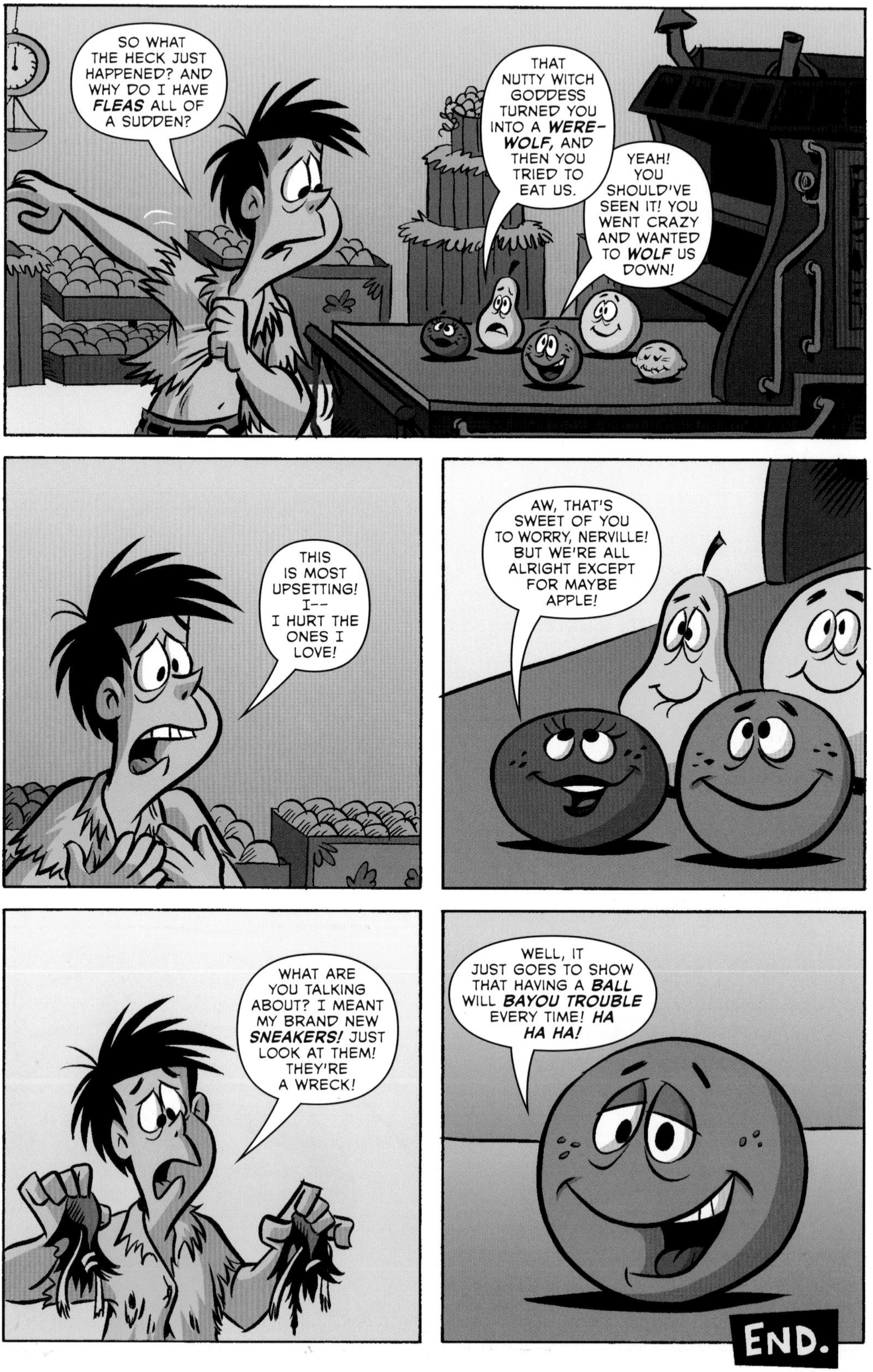
SO WHAT THE HECK JUST HAPPENED? AND WHY DO I HAVE FLEAS ALL OF A SUDDEN?
THAT NUTTY WITCH GODDESS TURNED YOU INTO A WERE-WOLF, AND THEN YOU TRIED TO EAT US.
YEAH! YOU SHOULD'VE SEEN IT! YOU WENT CRAZY AND WANTED TO WOLF US DOWN!
THIS IS MOST UPSETTING! I-- I HURT THE ONES I LOVE!
AW, THAT'S SWEET OF YOU TO WORRY, NERVILLE! BUT WE'RE ALL ALRIGHT EXCEPT FOR MAYBE APPLE!
WHAT ARE YOU TALKING ABOUT? I MEANT MY BRAND NEW SNEAKERS! JUST LOOK AT THEM! THEY'RE A WRECK!
WELL, IT JUST GOES TO SHOW THAT HAVING A BALL WILL BAYOU TROUBLE EVERY TIME! HA HA HA!
END.

JEEPERS, KIDS!

(PHONY ADVERTISEMENT)

RESIST THE CRUEL OPPRESSION OF THE KILLER MUTANT BRUSSEL SPROUTS with this KEEN-O ATOMIC PEA-SHOOTER!

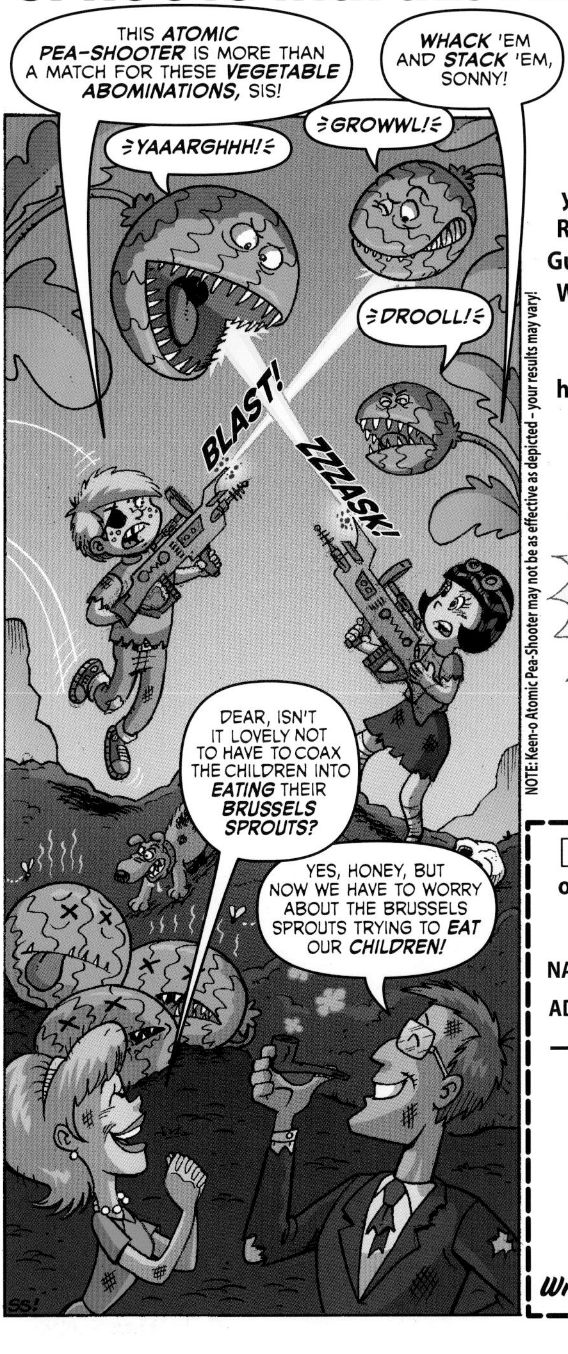
THIS ATOMIC PEA-SHOOTER IS MORE THAN A MATCH FOR THESE VEGETABLE ABOMINATIONS, SIS!
WHACK 'EM AND STACK 'EM, SONNY!
≷GROWWL!≶
≷YAAARGHHH!≶
≷DROOLL!≶
BLAST!
ZZZASK!
DEAR, ISN'T IT LOVELY NOT TO HAVE TO COAX THE CHILDREN INTO EATING THEIR BRUSSELS SPROUTS?
YES, HONEY, BUT NOW WE HAVE TO WORRY ABOUT THE BRUSSELS SPROUTS TRYING TO EAT OUR CHILDREN!
SS!

NOTE: Keen-o Atomic Pea-Shooter may not be as effective as depicted – your results may vary!

Remember Drekko industries' *HOME BOTANY LAB?* Remember how you and your friends all spawned your very own mutant Brussels sprouts? Remember how one of them ate your pet Guinea pig...? And then your grandmother? Well, it's time to fight back, with Drekko's atomic pea-shooter! Make those dirty sprouts pay for their crimes against humanity with this cool new high-impact plastic weapon!

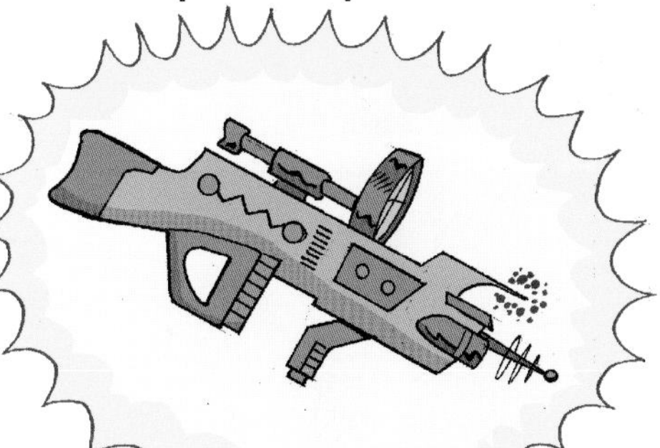

☐ ***Yes,*** **I can't wait to resist the cruel oppression of the killer mutant Brussels sprouts with your Keen-O Atomic Pea-shooter!**

NAME: ______________________

ADDRESS: ______________________

______________________ **ZIP CODE:** __________

Send this completed form along with ten rounds of ammo, plus three plasma grenades to cover postage and handling, to:

VEG-O-MANIC, INC.
19130 Duzzantexist Avenue
Fakeville, NY 11237

***Written and drawn by* SCOTT SHAW!**

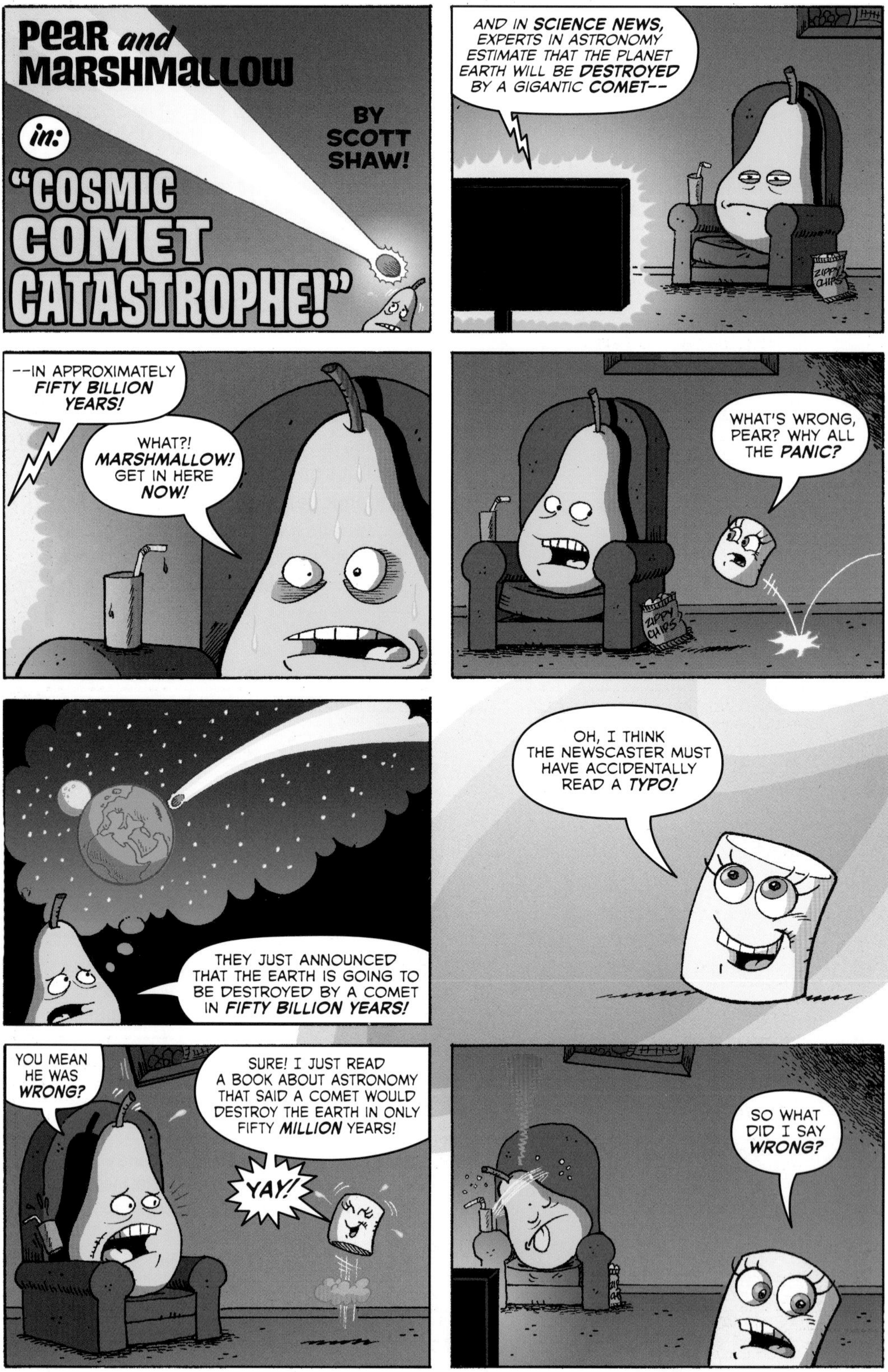
PEAR and MARSHMALLOW
in:
"COSMIC COMET CATASTROPHE!"
BY SCOTT SHAW!
AND IN SCIENCE NEWS, EXPERTS IN ASTRONOMY ESTIMATE THAT THE PLANET EARTH WILL BE DESTROYED BY A GIGANTIC COMET--
ZIPPY CHIPS
--IN APPROXIMATELY FIFTY BILLION YEARS!
WHAT?! MARSHMALLOW! GET IN HERE NOW!
WHAT'S WRONG, PEAR? WHY ALL THE PANIC?
ZIPPY CHIPS
THEY JUST ANNOUNCED THAT THE EARTH IS GOING TO BE DESTROYED BY A COMET IN FIFTY BILLION YEARS!
OH, I THINK THE NEWSCASTER MUST HAVE ACCIDENTALLY READ A TYPO!
YOU MEAN HE WAS WRONG?
SURE! I JUST READ A BOOK ABOUT ASTRONOMY THAT SAID A COMET WOULD DESTROY THE EARTH IN ONLY FIFTY MILLION YEARS!
YAY!
SO WHAT DID I SAY WRONG?

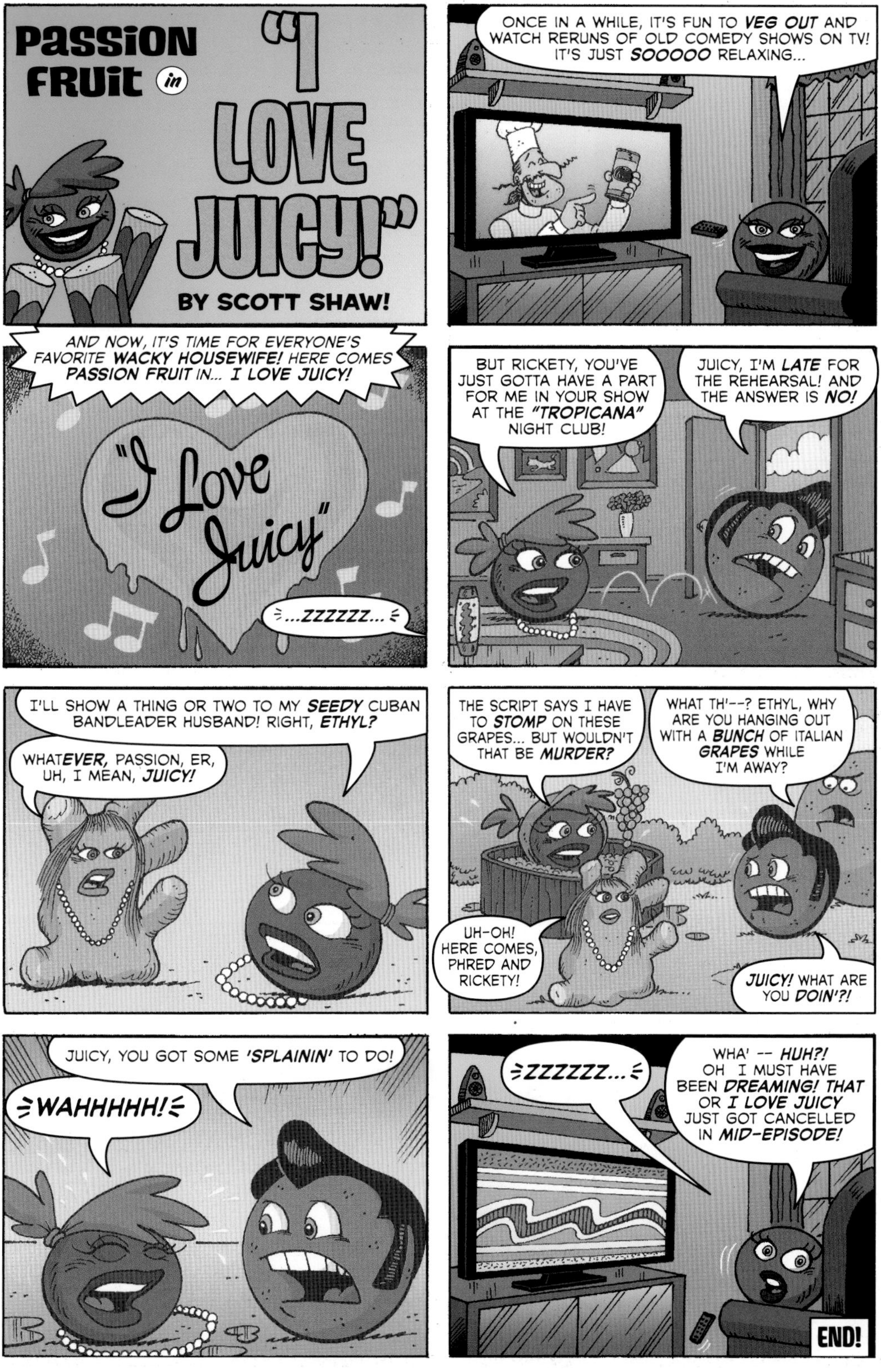
PASSION FRUIT in "I LOVE JUICY!"
BY SCOTT SHAW!
ONCE IN A WHILE, IT'S FUN TO VEG OUT AND WATCH RERUNS OF OLD COMEDY SHOWS ON TV! IT'S JUST SOOOOO RELAXING...
AND NOW, IT'S TIME FOR EVERYONE'S FAVORITE WACKY HOUSEWIFE! HERE COMES PASSION FRUIT IN... I LOVE JUICY!
"I Love Juicy"
...ZZZZZZ...
BUT RICKETY, YOU'VE JUST GOTTA HAVE A PART FOR ME IN YOUR SHOW AT THE "TROPICANA" NIGHT CLUB!
JUICY, I'M LATE FOR THE REHEARSAL! AND THE ANSWER IS NO!
I'LL SHOW A THING OR TWO TO MY SEEDY CUBAN BANDLEADER HUSBAND! RIGHT, ETHYL?
WHATEVER, PASSION, ER, UH, I MEAN, JUICY!
THE SCRIPT SAYS I HAVE TO STOMP ON THESE GRAPES... BUT WOULDN'T THAT BE MURDER?
WHAT TH'--? ETHYL, WHY ARE YOU HANGING OUT WITH A BUNCH OF ITALIAN GRAPES WHILE I'M AWAY?
UH-OH! HERE COMES, PHRED AND RICKETY!
JUICY! WHAT ARE YOU DOIN'?!
JUICY, YOU GOT SOME 'SPLAININ' TO DO!
WAHHHHH!
ZZZZZZ...
WHA' -- HUH?! OH I MUST HAVE BEEN DREAMING! THAT OR I LOVE JUICY JUST GOT CANCELLED IN MID-EPISODE!
END!

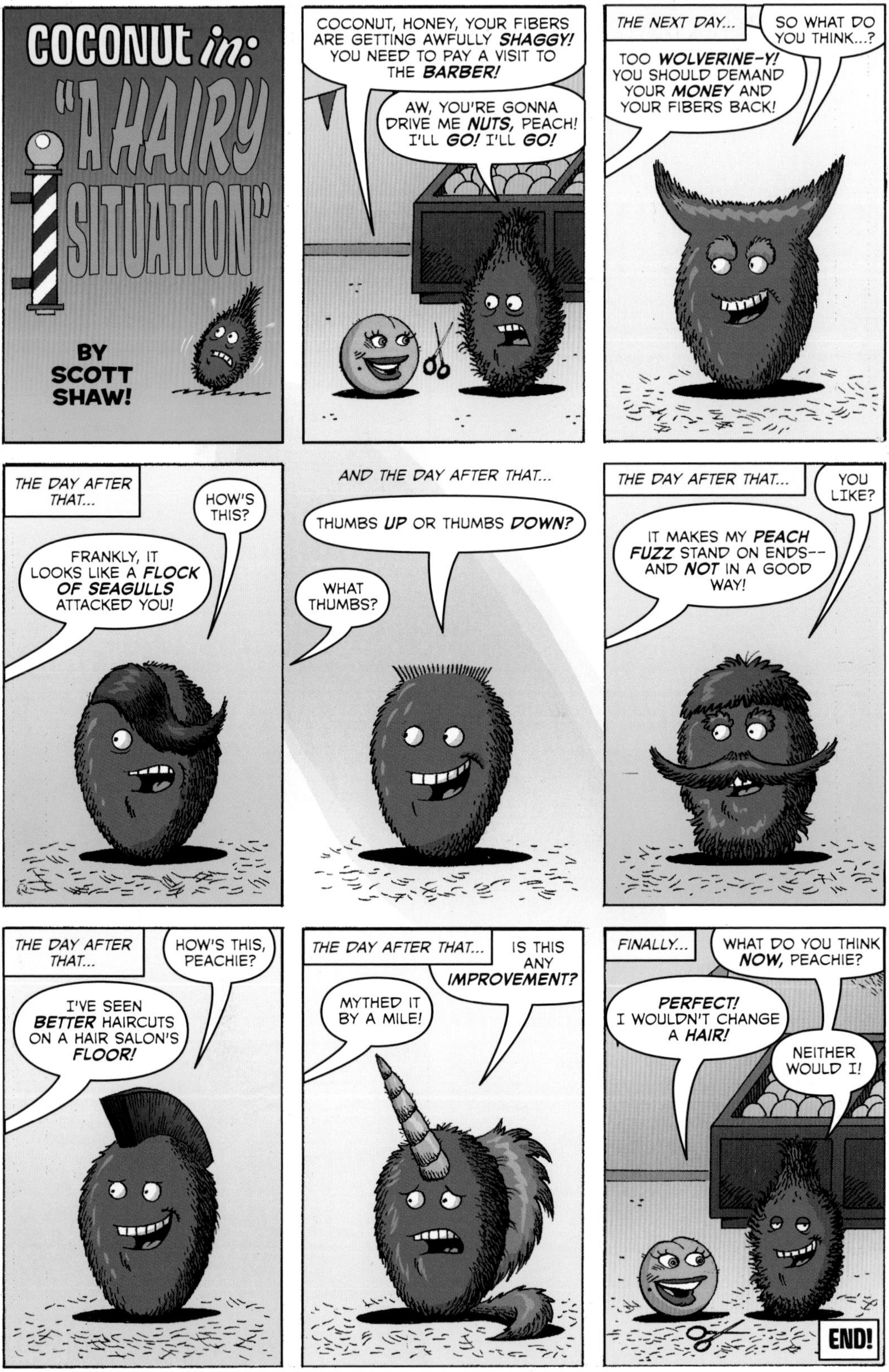
COCONUT in:
"A HAIRY SITUATION"
BY SCOTT SHAW!
COCONUT, HONEY, YOUR FIBERS ARE GETTING AWFULLY SHAGGY! YOU NEED TO PAY A VISIT TO THE BARBER!
AW, YOU'RE GONNA DRIVE ME NUTS, PEACH! I'LL GO! I'LL GO!
THE NEXT DAY...
SO WHAT DO YOU THINK...?
TOO WOLVERINE-Y! YOU SHOULD DEMAND YOUR MONEY AND YOUR FIBERS BACK!
THE DAY AFTER THAT...
HOW'S THIS?
FRANKLY, IT LOOKS LIKE A FLOCK OF SEAGULLS ATTACKED YOU!
AND THE DAY AFTER THAT...
THUMBS UP OR THUMBS DOWN?
WHAT THUMBS?
THE DAY AFTER THAT...
YOU LIKE?
IT MAKES MY PEACH FUZZ STAND ON ENDS-- AND NOT IN A GOOD WAY!
THE DAY AFTER THAT...
HOW'S THIS, PEACHIE?
I'VE SEEN BETTER HAIRCUTS ON A HAIR SALON'S FLOOR!
THE DAY AFTER THAT...
IS THIS ANY IMPROVEMENT?
MYTHED IT BY A MILE!
FINALLY...
WHAT DO YOU THINK NOW, PEACHIE?
PERFECT! I WOULDN'T CHANGE A HAIR!
NEITHER WOULD I!
END!

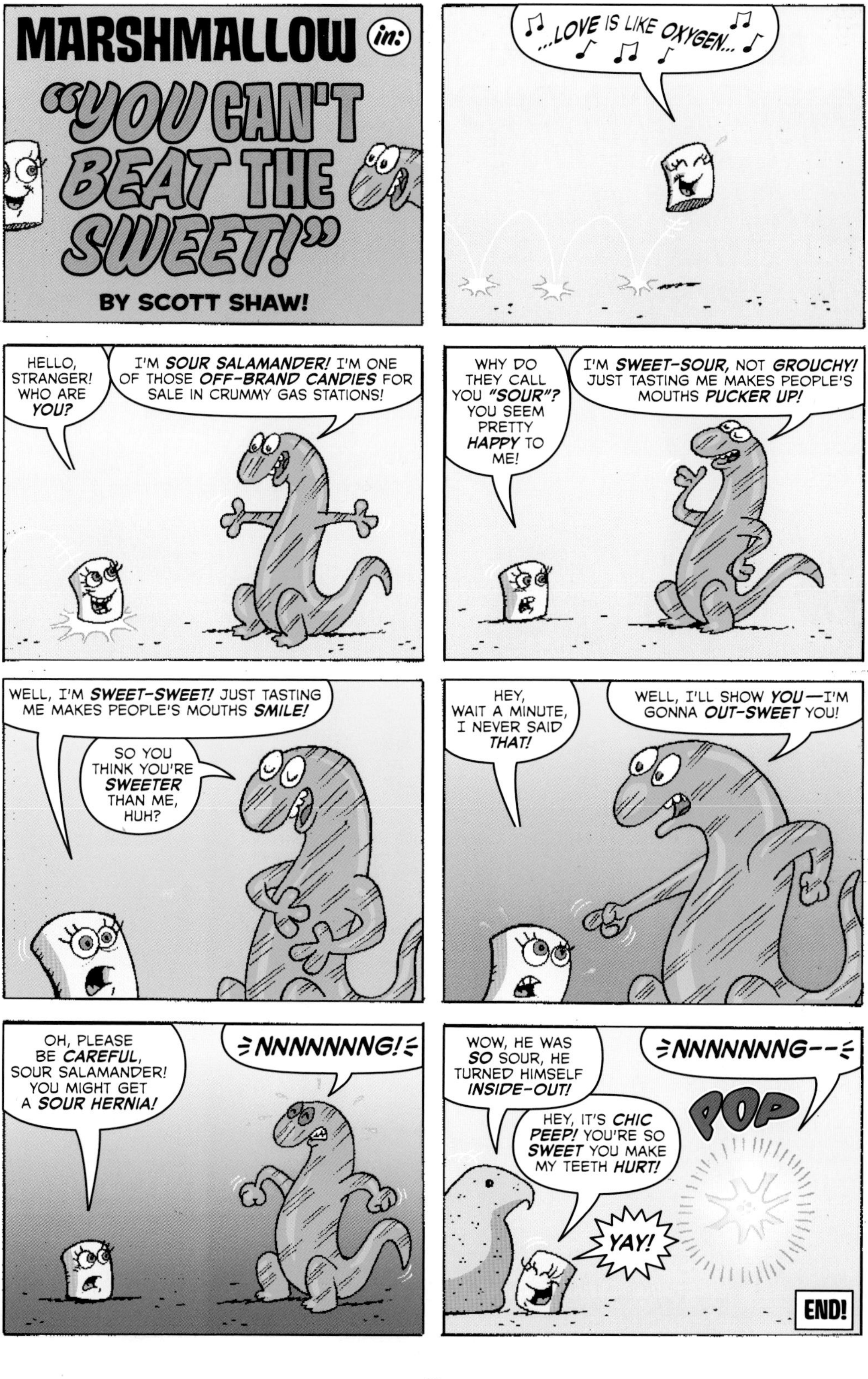
MARSHMALLOW in:
"YOU CAN'T BEAT THE SWEET!"
BY SCOTT SHAW!
...LOVE IS LIKE OXYGEN...
HELLO, STRANGER! WHO ARE YOU?
I'M SOUR SALAMANDER! I'M ONE OF THOSE OFF-BRAND CANDIES FOR SALE IN CRUMMY GAS STATIONS!
WHY DO THEY CALL YOU "SOUR"? YOU SEEM PRETTY HAPPY TO ME!
I'M SWEET-SOUR, NOT GROUCHY! JUST TASTING ME MAKES PEOPLE'S MOUTHS PUCKER UP!
WELL, I'M SWEET-SWEET! JUST TASTING ME MAKES PEOPLE'S MOUTHS SMILE!
SO YOU THINK YOU'RE SWEETER THAN ME, HUH?
HEY, WAIT A MINUTE, I NEVER SAID THAT!
WELL, I'LL SHOW YOU—I'M GONNA OUT-SWEET YOU!
OH, PLEASE BE CAREFUL, SOUR SALAMANDER! YOU MIGHT GET A SOUR HERNIA!
NNNNNNNG!
WOW, HE WAS SO SOUR, HE TURNED HIMSELF INSIDE-OUT!
NNNNNNNG--
POP
HEY, IT'S CHIC PEEP! YOU'RE SO SWEET YOU MAKE MY TEETH HURT!
YAY!
END!

GRANDPA LEMON in:
"PRAISING CAINE!"
BY SCOTT SHAW!

PASSION *FRUIT* GAVE ME ONE OF THESE FANCY, NEW-FANGLED *CANES*...

SALE!

SEE? THE *"STEADI-CANE"* HAS SPECIAL STRUTS THAT SUPPOSEDLY HELP OLD FOLK LIKE ME TO GET AROUND EASIER!

WHOA! THIS GADGET DOES TAKE A LITTLE GETTIN' *USED* TO!

WHOOPS! MAKE THAT A *LOT* OF GETTIN' USED TO!

AHHH! Y'KNOW, I THINK I'VE FINALLY *FIGURED OUT* HOW TO USE THIS TRICKY CANE!

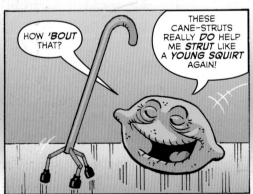

HOW *'BOUT* THAT?

THESE CANE-STRUTS REALLY *DO* HELP ME *STRUT* LIKE A *YOUNG SQUIRT* AGAIN!

YES, *SIR!* WATCH ME--

SQUISH

--AAAGH!

END!

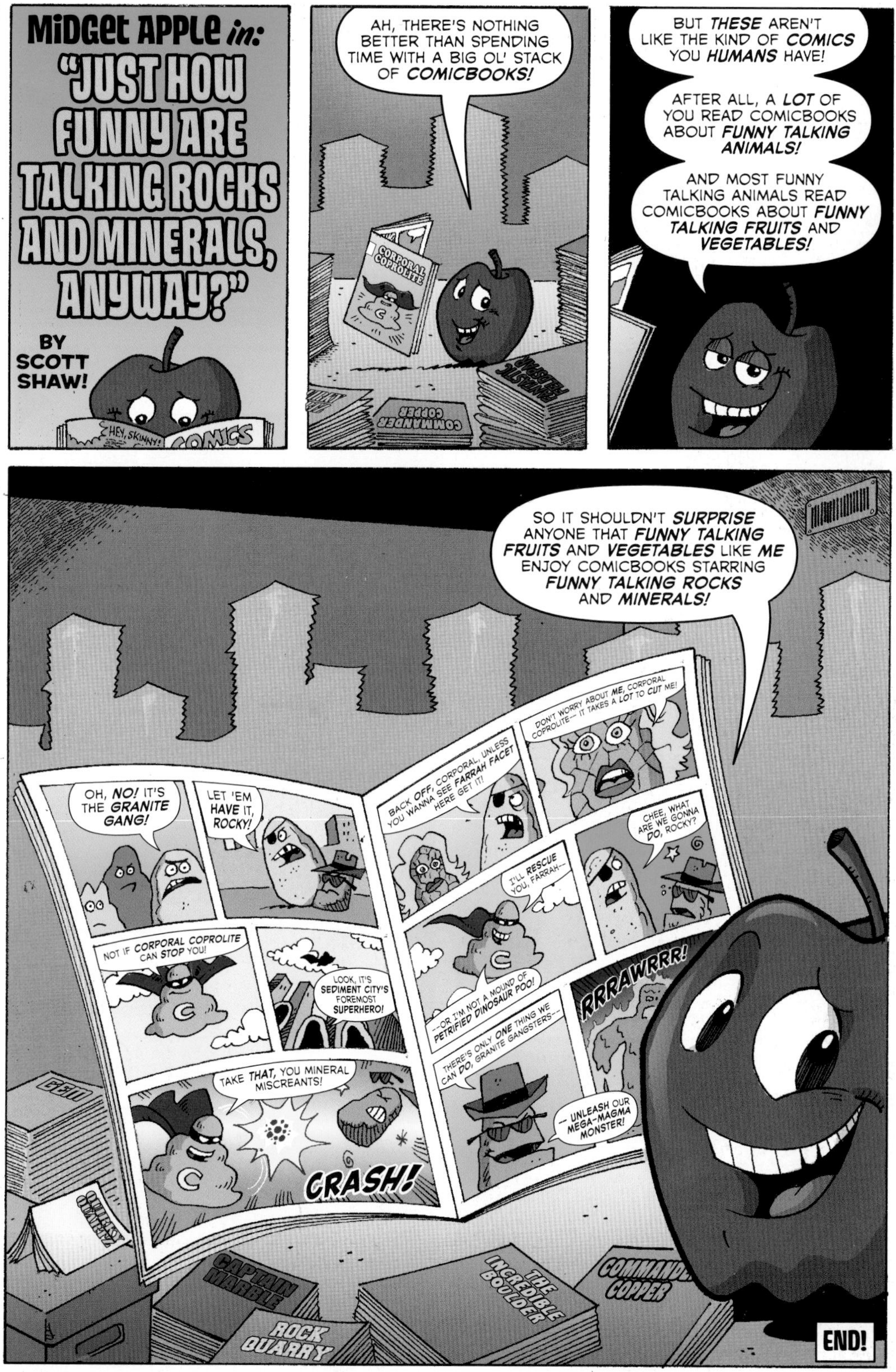
MIDGET APPLE in:
"JUST HOW FUNNY ARE TALKING ROCKS AND MINERALS, ANYWAY?"
BY SCOTT SHAW!
HEY, SKINNY!
COMICS
AH, THERE'S NOTHING BETTER THAN SPENDING TIME WITH A BIG OL' STACK OF COMICBOOKS!
CORPORAL COPROLITE
COMMANDER COPPER
BUT THESE AREN'T LIKE THE KIND OF COMICS YOU HUMANS HAVE!
AFTER ALL, A LOT OF YOU READ COMICBOOKS ABOUT FUNNY TALKING ANIMALS!
AND MOST FUNNY TALKING ANIMALS READ COMICBOOKS ABOUT FUNNY TALKING FRUITS AND VEGETABLES!
SO IT SHOULDN'T SURPRISE ANYONE THAT FUNNY TALKING FRUITS AND VEGETABLES LIKE ME ENJOY COMICBOOKS STARRING FUNNY TALKING ROCKS AND MINERALS!
OH, NO! IT'S THE GRANITE GANG!
LET 'EM HAVE IT, ROCKY!
NOT IF CORPORAL COPROLITE CAN STOP YOU!
LOOK, IT'S SEDIMENT CITY'S FOREMOST SUPERHERO!
TAKE THAT, YOU MINERAL MISCREANTS!
CRASH!
BACK OFF, CORPORAL, UNLESS YOU WANNA SEE FARRAH FACET HERE GET IT!
DON'T WORRY ABOUT ME, CORPORAL COPROLITE-- IT TAKES A LOT TO CUT ME!
I'LL RESCUE YOU, FARRAH--
--OR I'M NOT A MOUND OF PETRIFIED DINOSAUR POO!
CHEE, WHAT ARE WE GONNA DO, ROCKY?
THERE'S ONLY ONE THING WE CAN DO, GRANITE GANGSTERS--
-- UNLEASH OUR MEGA-MAGMA MONSTER!
RRRAWRRR!
CAPTAIN MARBLE
THE INCREDIBLE BOULDER
COMMANDER COPPER
ROCK QUARRY
END!

APPLE in:
"SUPER-SOUR SEMINAR!"
BY SCOTT SHAW!
EH, IT'S FREE, SO WHAT DO I HAVE TO LOSE?
FREE POSITIVE THINKING SEMINAR TODAY!
HOWDY! MY NAME'S NACHO McCHIP! HAVIN' FUN IS MY REASON FOR LIVING! ≶HAHAH!≷
HI! MY NAME'S HARDY THE PARTY HAT! "PARTY HARDY," GET IT? ≶CHUCKLE!≷
≶MUMBLE!≷ I'M APPLE. ≶GRUNT!≷
WELCOME TO MY SEMINAR ON POSITIVE THINKING! I'M DR. NORMAL VINCENT PEELER AND FIRST, I'D LIKE TO--
DR. PEELER, I'VE GOT A QUESTION FOR YOU--
DR. VINCENT NORMAL PEELER
--IS THIS SEMINAR FREE ONLY BECAUSE YOU PLAN TO SELL US COPIES OF YOUR LATEST BOOK?
OR IS THAT BIG STACK OF 'EM IN THE BACK OF THIS HALL JUST A COINCIDENCE?
SMILE-STONES
WELL, ER, I BROUGHT THEM ALONG JUST IN CASE ANY OF YOU WOULD LIKE TO READ FURTHER ON MY SUGGESTIONS FOR HOW TO MAINTAIN A POSITIVE ATTITUDE!
AND FOR A TIDY PROFIT RIGHT, "DOCTOR"?!
≶HARUMPH!≷ WELL, OF COURSE I'LL CLEAR A SMALL AMOUNT BUT...
YOU HEAR THAT?
HE'S PLAYING US FOR SUCKERS! IT'S A SCAM!
HIS LAST NAME'S PEELER! HE WANTS TO PEEL US! LET'S GET THE CREEP!
UH-OH! I'D BETTER GET OUTTA HERE!
SHEESH, WHAT A BUNCH OF SOUR GRAPES! EVEN I'M NICER THAN ANY OF THEM -- OF THAT, I'M POSITIVE!
FREE POSITIVE THINKING SEMINAR TODAY!
END!

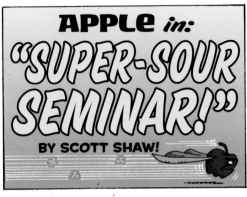

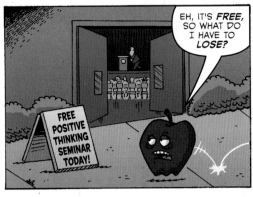

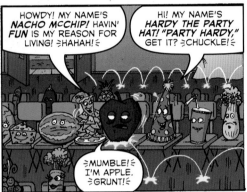

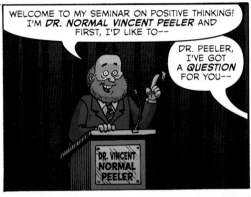

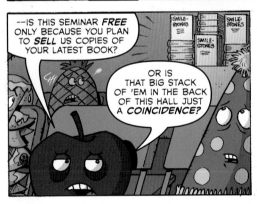

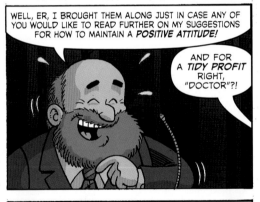

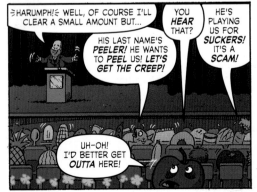

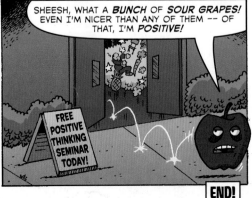

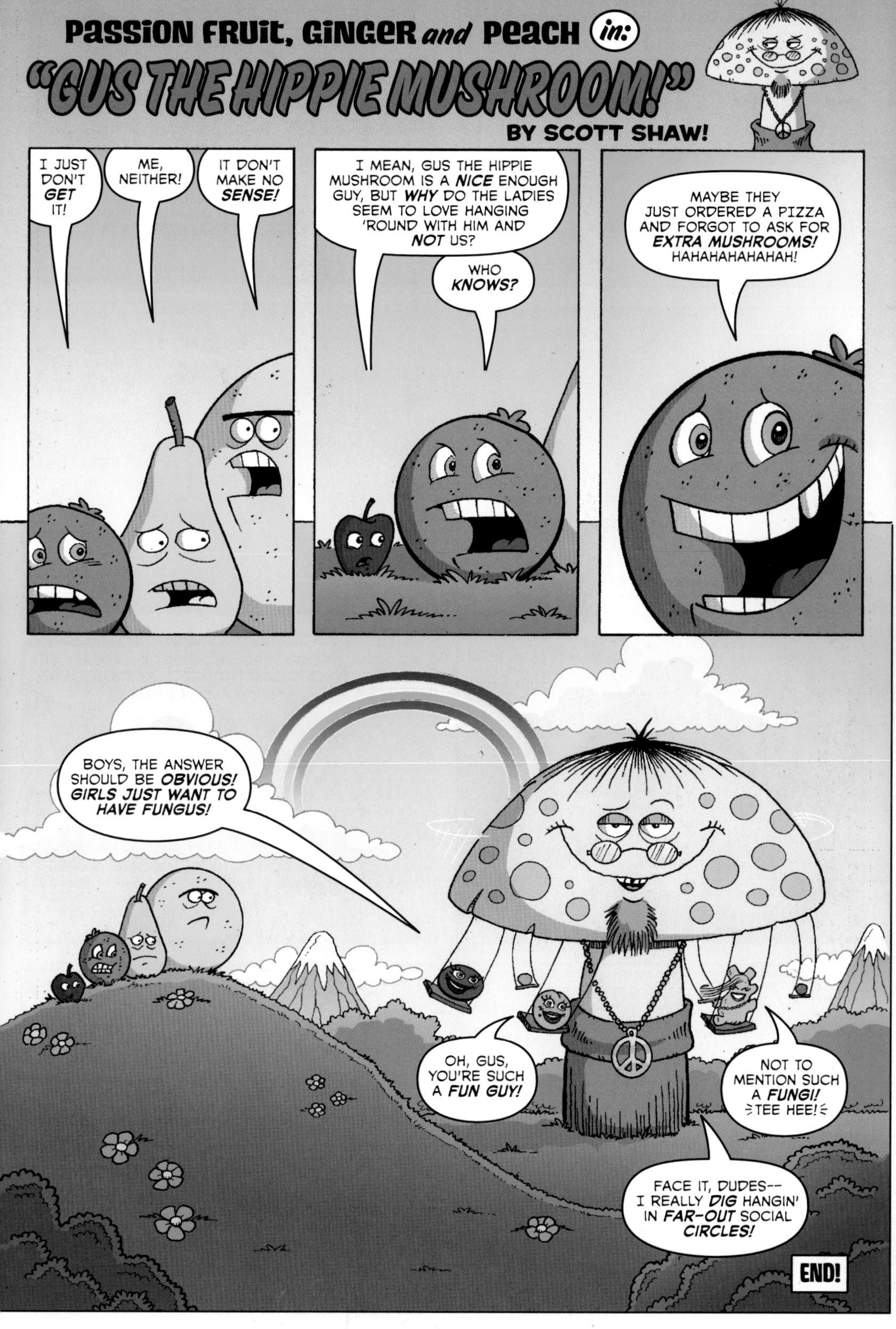
PASSION FRUIT, GINGER and PEACH in:
"GUS THE HIPPIE MUSHROOM!"
BY SCOTT SHAW!
I JUST DON'T GET IT!
ME, NEITHER!
IT DON'T MAKE NO SENSE!
I MEAN, GUS THE HIPPIE MUSHROOM IS A NICE ENOUGH GUY, BUT WHY DO THE LADIES SEEM TO LOVE HANGING 'ROUND WITH HIM AND NOT US?
WHO KNOWS?
MAYBE THEY JUST ORDERED A PIZZA AND FORGOT TO ASK FOR EXTRA MUSHROOMS! HAHAHAHAHAHAH!
BOYS, THE ANSWER SHOULD BE OBVIOUS! GIRLS JUST WANT TO HAVE FUNGUS!
OH, GUS, YOU'RE SUCH A FUN GUY!
NOT TO MENTION SUCH A FUNGI! TEE HEE!
FACE IT, DUDES-- I REALLY DIG HANGIN' IN FAR-OUT SOCIAL CIRCLES!
END!

EVIL ALIEN BROCCOLI OVERLORD in: "THE DAY THE FRUIT STOOD STILL!"

BY SCOTT SHAW!

FINALLY, I HAVE THE MEANS TO *CONQUER* THE PLANET *EARTH*-- AND CONQUER ANNOYING ORANGE AND HIS FRIENDS, TOO!

AFTER MONTHS OF RESEARCH AND DEVELOPMENT, I'VE DESIGNED THE *ULTIMATE WEAPON*--

--A FREEZE RAY THAT WILL PUT ALL OF EARTH'S INHABITANTS *ON ICE*-- *FOREVER!*

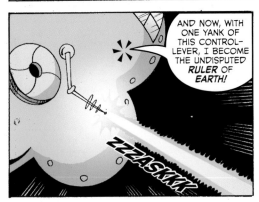

AND NOW, WITH ONE YANK OF THIS CONTROL-LEVER, I BECOME THE UNDISPUTED *RULER* OF *EARTH!*

ZZZASKKKK

AHHH, WHAT A COMFORTING SIGHT IT IS TO SEE ANNOYING ORANGE AND HIS ONLY SLIGHTLY-LESS-ANNOYING POSSE ETERNALLY TRAPPED IN A *FROZEN LIMBO!*

EXCUSE ME, SIR--

CADET, WHATEVER IT IS YOU HAVE TO TELL ME, IT HAD BETTER BE WORTH *INTERRUPTING* MY CROWNING MOMENT OF *TRIUMPH!*

SIR, THE *BAD* NEWS IS THAT THOSE MOTIONLESS IMAGES *AREN'T* ANNOYING ORANGE AND HIS FRIENDS! THEY'RE ACTUALLY *TOYS!*

-- AND THE *GOOD* NEWS, CADET?

WELL, THEY'RE ARE *ON SALE!*

°ANNOYING ORANGE° TOYS ON SALE -- **10% OFF!**

≈*YARRRGGGHHHHH!*≈

END!

WATCH OUT FOR PAPERCUTZ

Welcome to the fruit-filled fourth ANNOYING ORANGE graphic novel from Papercutz (the organization consisting of humans dedicated to creating great graphic novels for all ages). I'm Jim Saladcrop, er, Salicrup, the Editor-in-Cheese and Keeper of Grandpa Lemon's spectacles.

As a comicbook editor, I get to work with a lot of very interesting and creative people. For example, we'll soon be launching a new comic called WWE SUPERSTARS, published under our new imprint "Super Genius," and it's written by Mick Foley—the three-time WWE Champion, the Hardcore Legend, and a New York Times best-selling author. Turns out Mick is a big comics fan and he's thrilled to write our new series. So how cool is it to work with a guy like that? Especially for a long-time Wrestling fan like myself? I'll tell you—VERY cool!

Likewise when we were searching for the right talent to write and draw ANNOYING ORANGE, we didn't have to look far. Working on the Cartoon Network TV series creating storyboards and writing gags were none other than two of the best comicbook talents around—Mike Kazaleh and Scott Shaw! Not only do they both wear Hawaiian shirts (part of the official uniform of Californian animators), contribute to THE SIMPSONS comics, but they both drew funny animal Captains-- Mike created the feline Captain Jack and Scott co-created (with Roy Thomas) the rabbit Captain Carrot. I'm a big fan of both of these guys, and just as I'm excited to work with Mick Foley, I'm also thrilled to work with two of the best cartoonists working in comics today! (Speaking of which, check out the pic of me with a few of my cartooning gods!)

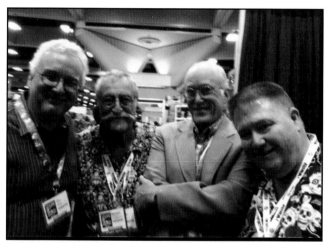

From left to right: Jim Salicrup, MAD's Serio Aragones, UNCLE SCROOGE's Don Rosa, and Scott Shaw! at the 2013 Comic-Con International: Sandy-Eggo, er, San Diego.

Since the first graphic novel, Mike and Scott have each written and drawn half of each book, alternating who would write and draw the cover feature. So while Mike created "Chilli Chiller," Scott decided to fill the rest of the book up with single pages of comics, puzzles, and phony ads. I think it was Scott's sneaky way to get his name plastered all over this book! Speaking of those puzzles, here're the answers to the "Crossword Fun with Fruit!" crossword puzzle (You're on your own with the other puzzles!):

1 G	2 R	3 A	4 P	5 E	■	■
■	6 F	R	U	I	T	■
7 I	S	■	■	■	■	8 A
■	■	9 B	I	G	■	■
10 F	11 A	T	■	■	■	■
■	12 S	O	13 U	14 R	■	■
■	■	■	15 P	U	S	S

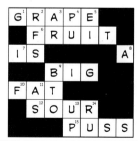

Scott's come up with another crazy idea for ANNOYING ORANGE #7, but we don't want to spoil the surprise, so you'll just have to wait for it. Just as you'll have to wait for ANNOYING ORANGE #5 "Transfarmers: Fruit Processors in Disguise" coming soon! Until then, keep on watching ANNOYING ORANGE on Cartoon Network and YouTube!

Thanks,

Jim

STAY IN TOUCH!

EMAIL:	salicrup@papercutz.com
WEB:	www.papercutz.com
TWITTER:	@papercutzgn
FACEBOOK:	PAPERCUTZGRAPHICNOVELS
REGULAR MAIL:	Papercutz, 160 Broadway, Suite 700, East Wing, New York, NY 10038

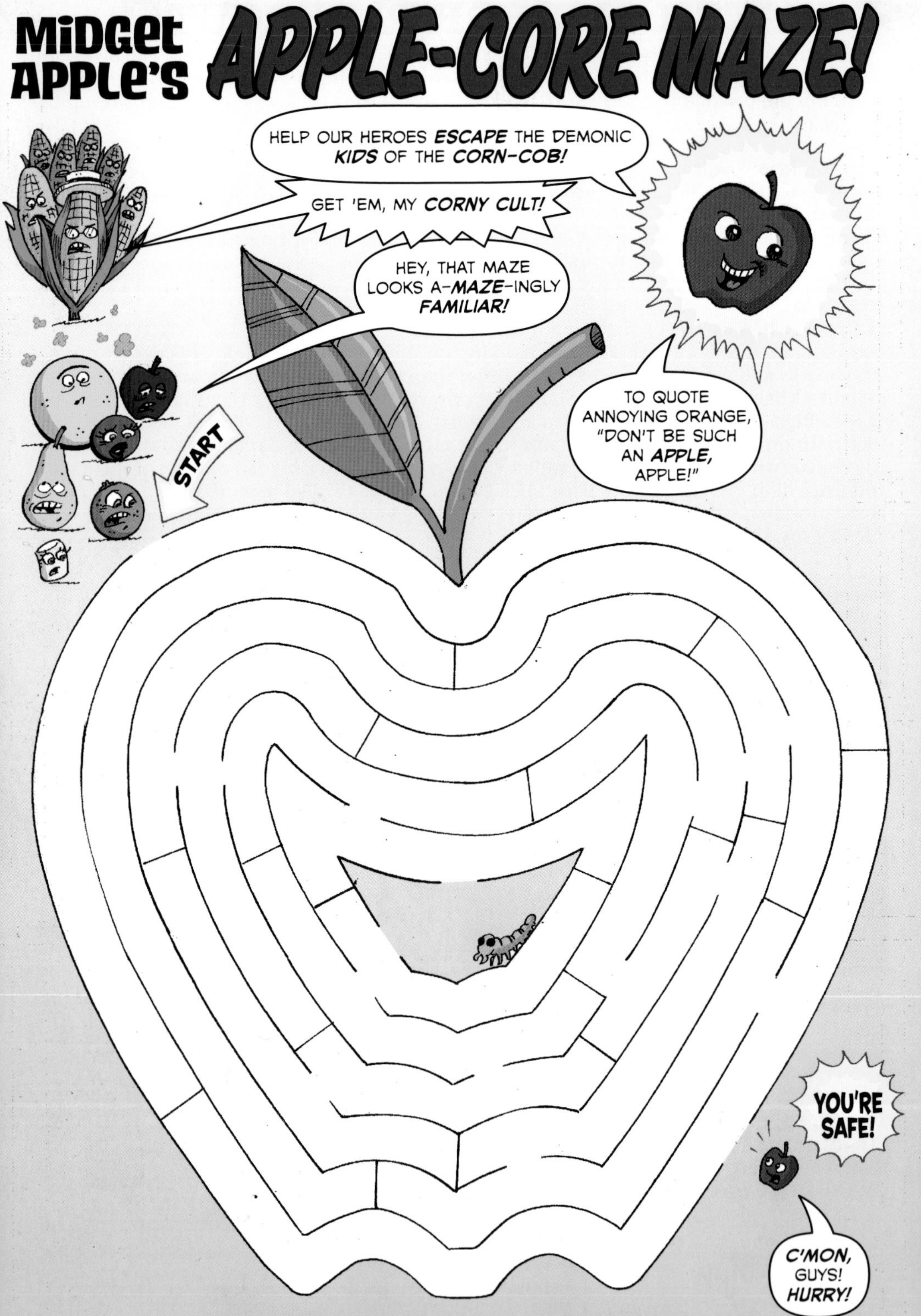
MIDGET APPLE'S APPLE-CORE MAZE!
HELP OUR HEROES ESCAPE THE DEMONIC KIDS OF THE CORN-COB!
GET 'EM, MY CORNY CULT!
HEY, THAT MAZE LOOKS A-MAZE-INGLY FAMILIAR!
TO QUOTE ANNOYING ORANGE, "DON'T BE SUCH AN APPLE, APPLE!"
START
YOU'RE SAFE!
C'MON, GUYS! HURRY!

WRITTEN AND DRAWN BY SCOTT SHAW!

DANE BOEDIGHEIMER

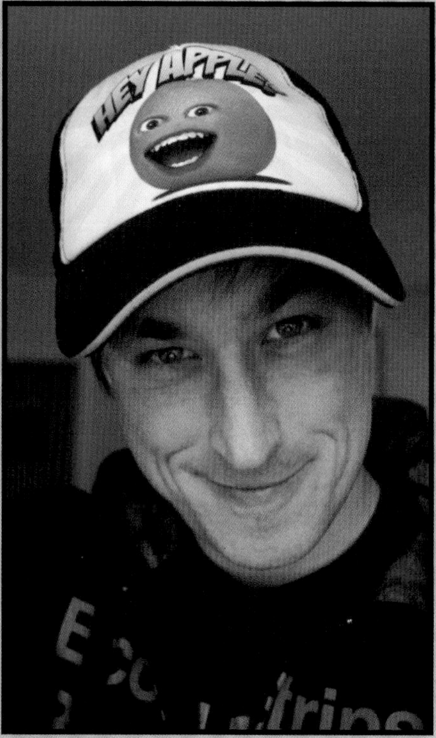

Dane (or Daneboe as he's known online) is a filmmaker and goofball extraordinaire. Dane spent most of his life in the glamorous Midwest, Harwood, North Dakota, to be exact. With nothing better to do, (it was North Dakota) at around the age of twelve, Dane began making short movies and videos with his parents' camcorder. Since then he has made hundreds, if not thousands of short web videos… many of which are only funny to him. But Dane has remained determined to make "the perfect short comedy film;" one that will end all social problems and bring laughter to all the children of the world.

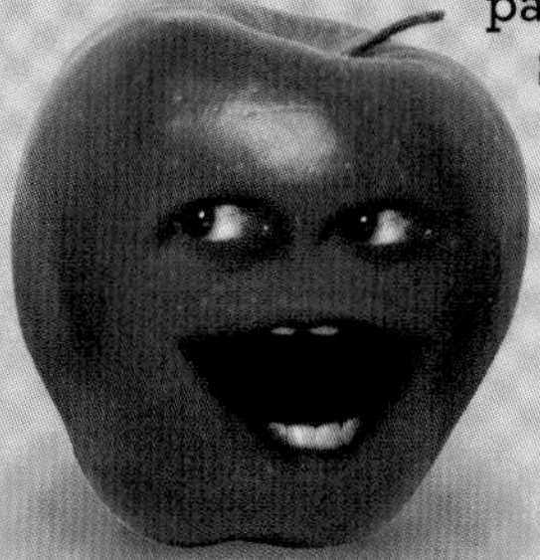

Currently, Dane is most widely known for creating The Annoying Orange, one of the most successful web series ever. The Annoying Orange has over 2 million subscribers and over 1 billion video views on YouTube as well as over 11 million facebook fans. On top of that, The Annoying Orange has a top rated show on Cartoon Network! As a result, fans have clamored for all sorts of cool Annoying Orange toys, t-shirts, games, etc. And despite all the wonderful stuff that has already appeared, fans still want more, and we suspect they'll be getting it.

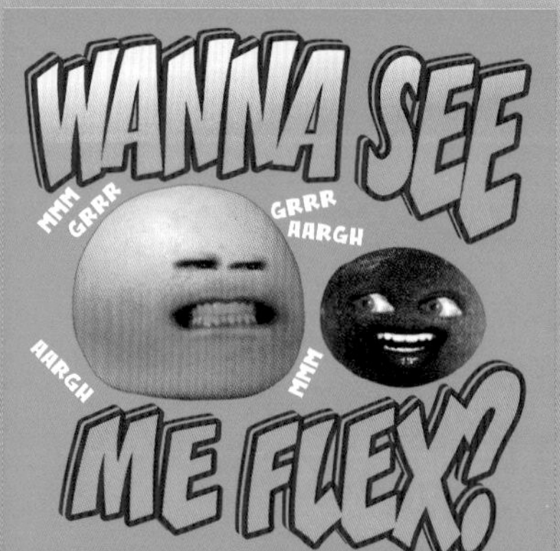
WANNA SEE
MMM
GRRR
GRRR
AARGH
AARGH
MMM
ME FLEX?

Not to be completely undone, Dane's other videos have been viewed over 650 million times and have been featured on TV, as well as some of the most popular entertainment, news, and video sharing sites on the Internet.

In Dane's downtime he enjoys… oh, who are we kidding? Dane doesn't have any downtime. He wouldn't know what to do with himself if he did.

SPENCER GROVE

Spencer Grove has written plays, prose, television scripts and more online videos than any sane person should attempt. Also, he bakes a mean apple pie.

He began his career in independent productions, working on everything from infomercials to award shows, eventually moving to MTV where he served as an Associate Producer on Pimp My Ride. Since 2009, he has served as the head writer of the Annoying Orange web series, creating and co-creating the supporting cast and developing the ever-expanding online world of the Orange.

TOM SHEPPARD

Tom Sheppard is a multiple Emmy-award winning talking animal wordsmith. He's written for all manner of beasts, from genetically altered lab mice, to crazy barnyard animals, butt-obsessed monkeys and even the occasional human, such as the Green Lantern. Since diving into the world of Annoying Orange, it has been his pleasure to expand his repertoire to talking fruit. He is currently writing, producing and directing the live action/animated High Fructose Adventures of Annoying Orange for Cartoon Network.

MIKE KAZALEH

Mike Kazaleh is a veteran of comicbooks and animated cartoons. He began his career producing low budget commercials and sales films out of his tiny studio in Detroit, Michigan. Mike soon moved to Los Angeles, California and since then he has worked for most of the major cartoon studios and comicbook companies.

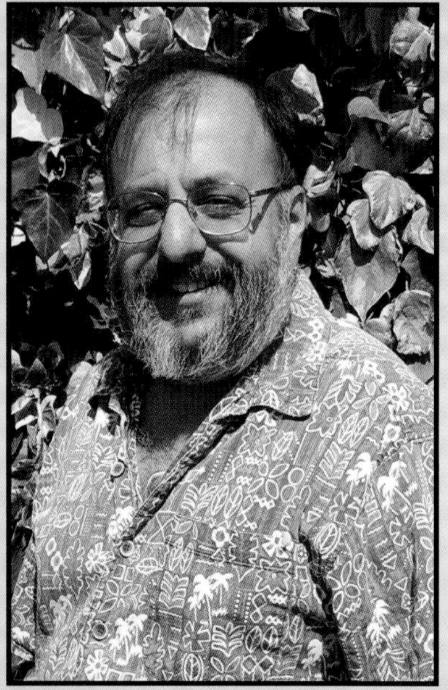

He has worked with such characters as The Flintstones, The Simpsons, Mighty Mouse, Krypto the Superdog, Ren and Stimpy, Cow and Chicken, and Bugs Bunny, as well as creating his own independent comics including THE ADVENTURES OF CAPTAIN JACK. Before all this stuff happened, Mike was a TV repairman.

ANNOYING ORANGE in:
"BOYS vs. GIRLS"

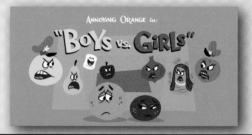

Above: A title card designed by Mike Kazaleh.

SCOTT SHAW!

Scott Shaw! is an award-winning cartoonist/writer of comicbooks, animation, advertising, toy design, and a historian of all forms of cartooning. Scott was also one of the comics fans who organized the first San Diego Comic-Con, where he has become known for performing his hilarious ODDBALL COMICS slide show. www.shawcartoons.com. Check out the comic on the next page for Scott's cartoon version of an early encounter with a comicbook legend.

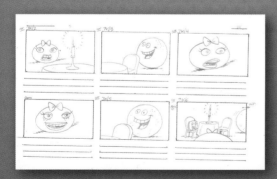

Above: an example of Scott's storyboards for the ANNOYING ORANGE TV series

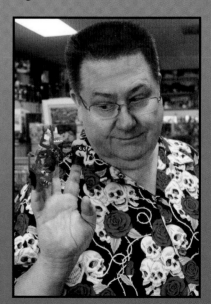

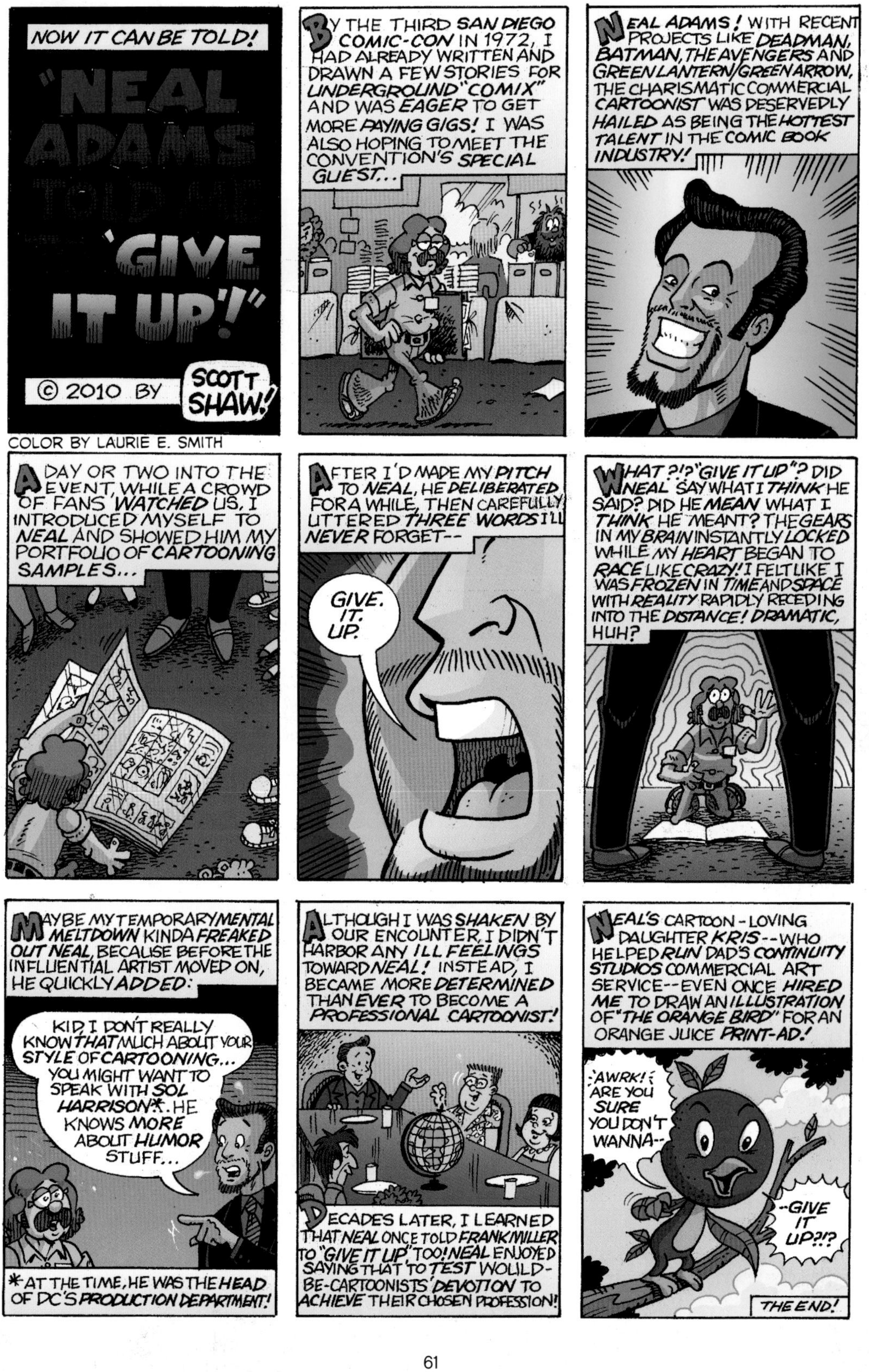
NOW IT CAN BE TOLD!
"NEAL ADAMS TOLD ME 'GIVE IT UP'!"
© 2010 BY SCOTT SHAW!
COLOR BY LAURIE E. SMITH
BY THE THIRD SAN DIEGO COMIC-CON IN 1972, I HAD ALREADY WRITTEN AND DRAWN A FEW STORIES FOR UNDERGROUND "COMIX" AND WAS EAGER TO GET MORE PAYING GIGS! I WAS ALSO HOPING TO MEET THE CONVENTION'S SPECIAL GUEST...
NEAL ADAMS! WITH RECENT PROJECTS LIKE DEADMAN, BATMAN, THE AVENGERS AND GREEN LANTERN/GREEN ARROW, THE CHARISMATIC COMMERCIAL CARTOONIST WAS DESERVEDLY HAILED AS BEING THE HOTTEST TALENT IN THE COMIC BOOK INDUSTRY!
A DAY OR TWO INTO THE EVENT, WHILE A CROWD OF FANS WATCHED US, I INTRODUCED MYSELF TO NEAL AND SHOWED HIM MY PORTFOLIO OF CARTOONING SAMPLES...
AFTER I'D MADE MY PITCH TO NEAL, HE DELIBERATED FOR A WHILE, THEN CAREFULLY UTTERED THREE WORDS I'LL NEVER FORGET--
GIVE. IT. UP.
WHAT?!?"GIVE IT UP"? DID NEAL SAY WHAT I THINK HE SAID? DID HE MEAN WHAT I THINK HE MEANT? THE GEARS IN MY BRAIN INSTANTLY LOCKED WHILE MY HEART BEGAN TO RACE LIKE CRAZY! I FELT LIKE I WAS FROZEN IN TIME AND SPACE WITH REALITY RAPIDLY RECEDING INTO THE DISTANCE! DRAMATIC, HUH?
MAYBE MY TEMPORARY MENTAL MELTDOWN KINDA FREAKED OUT NEAL, BECAUSE BEFORE THE INFLUENTIAL ARTIST MOVED ON, HE QUICKLY ADDED:
KID, I DON'T REALLY KNOW THAT MUCH ABOUT YOUR STYLE OF CARTOONING... YOU MIGHT WANT TO SPEAK WITH SOL HARRISON*. HE KNOWS MORE ABOUT HUMOR STUFF...
*AT THE TIME, HE WAS THE HEAD OF DC'S PRODUCTION DEPARTMENT!
ALTHOUGH I WAS SHAKEN BY OUR ENCOUNTER, I DIDN'T HARBOR ANY ILL FEELINGS TOWARD NEAL! INSTEAD, I BECAME MORE DETERMINED THAN EVER TO BECOME A PROFESSIONAL CARTOONIST!
DECADES LATER, I LEARNED THAT NEAL ONCE TOLD FRANK MILLER TO "GIVE IT UP," TOO! NEAL ENJOYED SAYING THAT TO TEST WOULD-BE-CARTOONISTS' DEVOTION TO ACHIEVE THEIR CHOSEN PROFESSION!
NEAL'S CARTOON-LOVING DAUGHTER KRIS--WHO HELPED RUN DAD'S CONTINUITY STUDIOS COMMERCIAL ART SERVICE--EVEN ONCE HIRED ME TO DRAW AN ILLUSTRATION OF "THE ORANGE BIRD" FOR AN ORANGE JUICE PRINT-AD!
AWRK! ARE YOU SURE YOU DON'T WANNA--
--GIVE IT UP?!?
THE END!

NERVILLE *and* MARSHMALLOW'S
CONNECT-THE-DOTS PUZZLE!

FOR ***SHARP-MINDED*** FANS OF ANNOYING ORANGE!

WRITTEN AND DRAWN BY SCOTT SHAW!

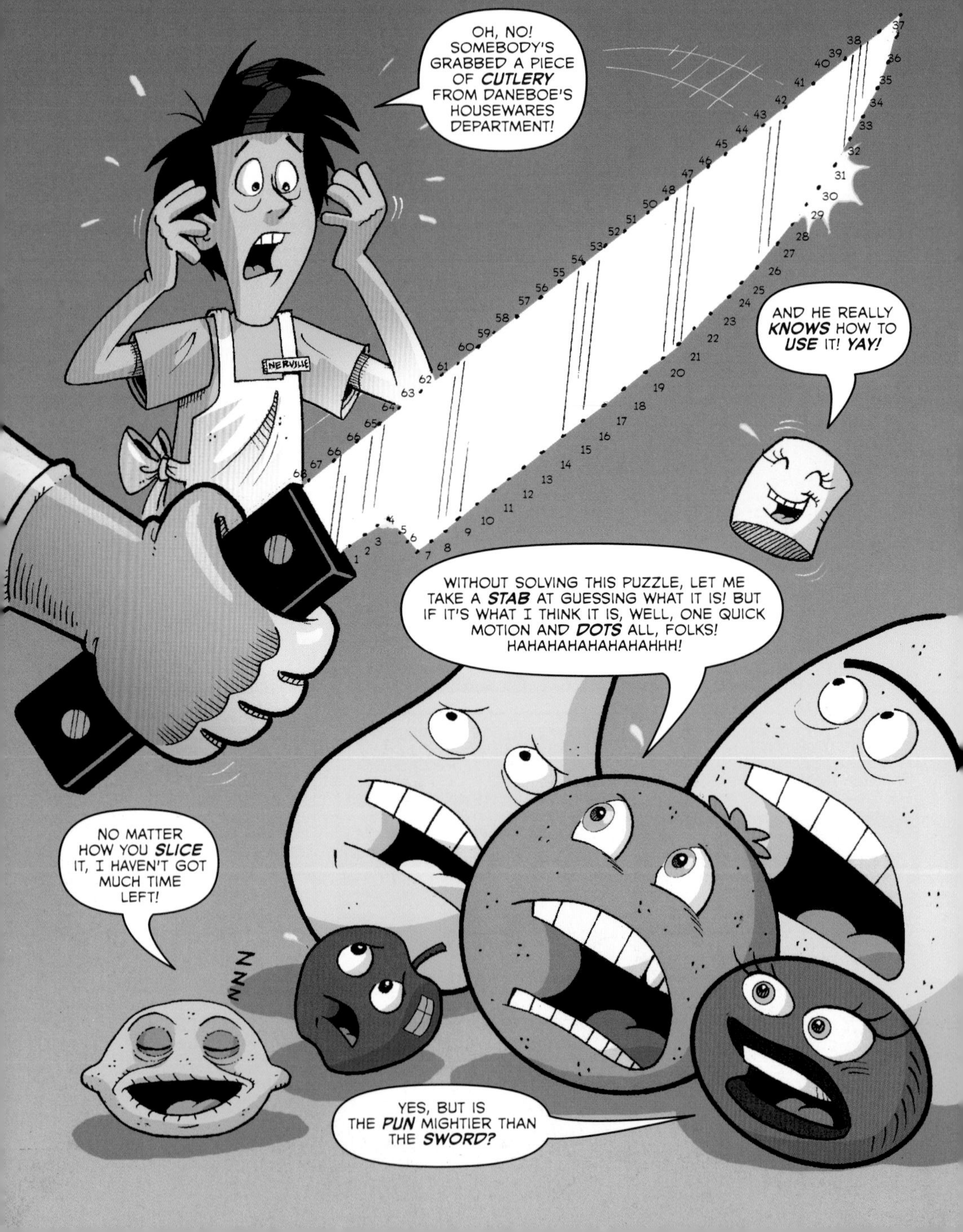

OH, NO! SOMEBODY'S GRABBED A PIECE OF CUTLERY FROM DANEBOE'S HOUSEWARES DEPARTMENT!
AND HE REALLY KNOWS HOW TO USE IT! YAY!
WITHOUT SOLVING THIS PUZZLE, LET ME TAKE A STAB AT GUESSING WHAT IT IS! BUT IF IT'S WHAT I THINK IT IS, WELL, ONE QUICK MOTION AND DOTS ALL, FOLKS! HAHAHAHAHAHAHAHHH!
NO MATTER HOW YOU SLICE IT, I HAVEN'T GOT MUCH TIME LEFT!
YES, BUT IS THE PUN MIGHTIER THAN THE SWORD?

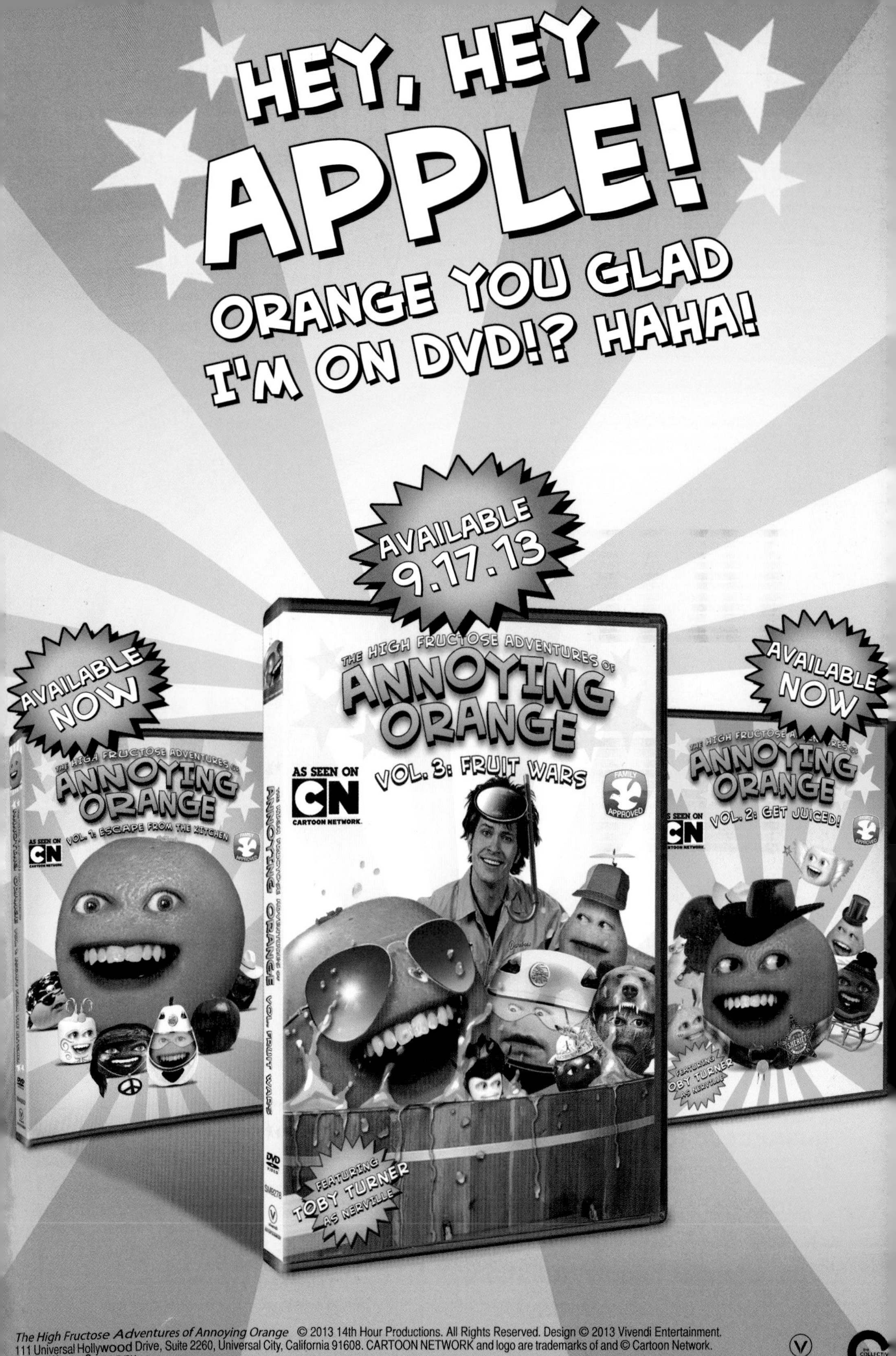
HEY, HEY
APPLE!
ORANGE YOU GLAD
I'M ON DVD!? HAHA!
AVAILABLE NOW
THE HIGH FRUCTOSE ADVENTURES OF
ANNOYING ORANGE
VOL. 1: ESCAPE FROM THE KITCHEN
AVAILABLE 9.17.13
THE HIGH FRUCTOSE ADVENTURES OF
ANNOYING ORANGE
AS SEEN ON
CN
CARTOON NETWORK
VOL. 3: FRUIT WARS
FAMILY APPROVED
FEATURING
TOBY TURNER
AS NERVILLE
AVAILABLE NOW
ANNOYING ORANGE
VOL. 2: GET JUICED!
FEATURING TOBY TURNER AS NERVILLE

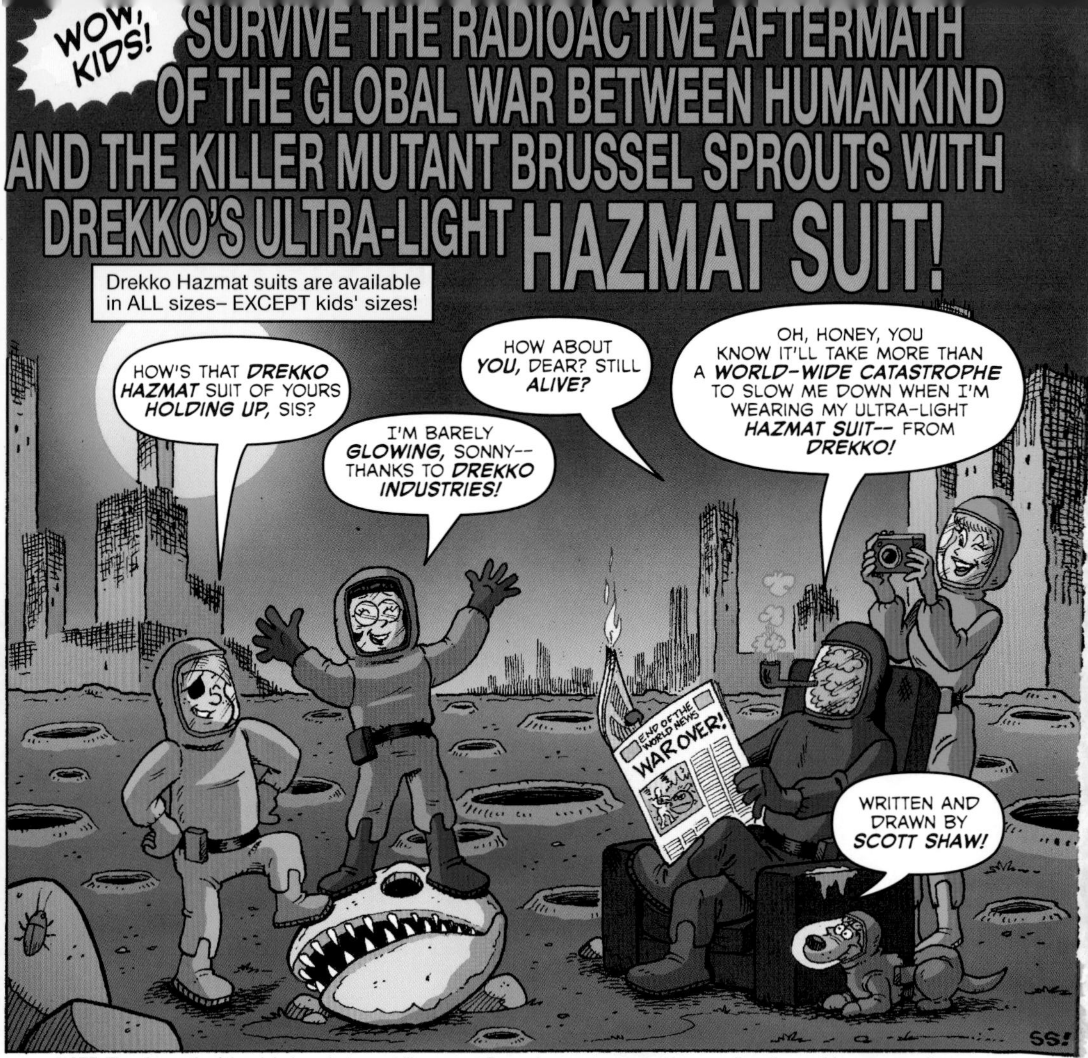
WOW, KIDS!
SURVIVE THE RADIOACTIVE AFTERMATH OF THE GLOBAL WAR BETWEEN HUMANKIND AND THE KILLER MUTANT BRUSSEL SPROUTS WITH DREKKO'S ULTRA-LIGHT HAZMAT SUIT!
Drekko Hazmat suits are available in ALL sizes– EXCEPT kids' sizes!
HOW'S THAT DREKKO HAZMAT SUIT OF YOURS HOLDING UP, SIS?
I'M BARELY GLOWING, SONNY-- THANKS TO DREKKO INDUSTRIES!
HOW ABOUT YOU, DEAR? STILL ALIVE?
OH, HONEY, YOU KNOW IT'LL TAKE MORE THAN A WORLD-WIDE CATASTROPHE TO SLOW ME DOWN WHEN I'M WEARING MY ULTRA-LIGHT HAZMAT SUIT-- FROM DREKKO!
END OF THE WORLD NEWS
WAR OVER!
WRITTEN AND DRAWN BY SCOTT SHAW!
SS!

NOTE: The aftermath of the global war between killer mutant Brussels sprouts may not be as radioactive as this – your results may vary!

Now, from their secret, lead-lined underground corporate headquarters, Drekko Industries is proud to announce their new line of ultra-light Hazmat suits, guaranteed to protect you from most microbes, bacteria, viruses and other forms of biological warfare! Each suit eliminates over 78% of most deadly radiation, too! Get yours today!

☐ **Yes,** I can't wait to survive the radioactive aftermath of the global war between humankind and the killer mutant Brussels sprouts with your ultra-light Hazmat suit!

NAME: ______________________________

ADDRESS: ___________________________

______________________ ZIP CODE: ________

Send this completed form along with two cans of untainted food, plus a roll of toilet paper for postage and handling, to:
VEG-O-MANIC, INC.
Third crater from the left
What's left of Fakeville, NY 11237

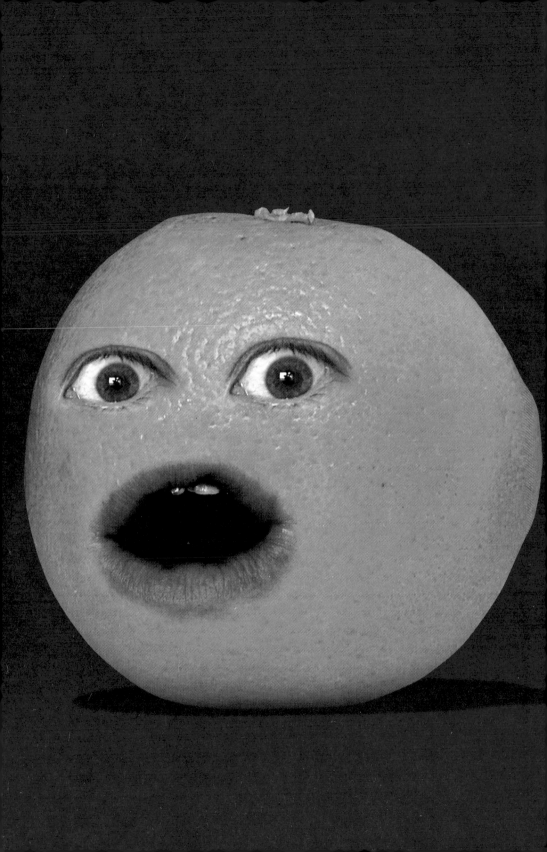